When The Whistler Calls

Also by Carla Day

One Leg Out

Scintillation (Short Story)

Colours of Her Rainbow

Forthcoming

The Bench

For Tom

My son, my world, my inspiration and my sunshine.

"When you have eliminated the impossible, whatever remains, however improbable, must be the truth."

Sherlock Holmes.

Acknowledgements

Thank you to all those who helped with the writing process of this book.

Most of all to my family, for losing me to the writing void for almost a year

Celeste J Heery, for the use of her brilliant artwork.

Thank you to the countless beta readers, who were invaluable.

Also, to my dear friend and advisor, Fai Jevons, who helped me see things more clearly. It's always good to have that one person who has your back.

And to those that I haven't named, thank you. You helped to make this book what it is.

WHEN THE WHISTLER CALLS

Carla Day

Published in 2022 by Carla J Day

Photography ~ Celeste J Heery
Graphic Art and Cover Design ~ Fai Jevons
Edited by ~ Fai Jevons

Third Edition

ISBN: 9798410283885

Chapters

ONE ~ Funerals

Burry Port, Wales, 2018.

Today is about lies and counterfeit smiles. Lilies have always been my favourite flower. David used to buy them for me on his way home from business trips that kept him away for half of the year. I like how big and bold they are, and how they curl like giant wood shavings, bringing to mind a feeling of childhood I could never really describe. A withered memory that was always on the verge of making its debut. The flowers seemed to make a statement and fill my conservatory with cheer. Today, however, I have a whole downstairs brimming with white lilies that seem to speak an altogether different language, to joyful. A language of truth, buried among lies, and a darkness that is hidden in the shadows of a previous life. One I'm going to have to face, but not today.

***

Black-clad bodies are milling around, drinking and eating in my kitchen as if it were an ordinary day. I don't remember a word said at the memorial service earlier, only soft mutterings and the distant sound of sobs, shoulders shaking, and crumpled tissues wiping away tears, some genuine, some obligatory.

So many people filled the intimate church that they spilled onto the street. The same old stone church we were married in twelve years ago. I don't think I cried. I haven't since the day I got the life changing phone call. I keep asking myself, *"Is that wrong?"* Should I be intermittently wailing and sitting amid a pyramid of tissues in my pyjamas with a sore nose and red eyes. Should I be doing something to outwardly show my grief? I'm sure I should, but I sincerely don't know how.

There's a part of me that doesn't know how to deal with this stuff. I'm not entirely sure how to act. This is new. David always advised me how to be appropriate in these kinds of sad situations, because my normal reaction would be to giggle or remain numb, like my emotions had been switched off; when in truth, there just aren't any. This is not out of disrespect to the deceased of course but borne from nerves and a genuine fear of people's reactions.

I wish David were here to save me from these maudlin crowds. Do I even know all these people? I don't think I do, save for immediate family and friends. The others could be anybody, random passers-by, come in from the street for a free drink and a few nibbles.

I remember focusing on a dark-blue car parked under the shade of an oak tree as we arrived at the church. We were in the limo, Lucinda was smoothing my hand, comforting me, as my eyes settled on a woman sitting inside. Her face partially hidden by the sun on the window screen, her gloved hand resting on the steering wheel. She was blowing smoke out of an opened window. I wondered who she was there for, which member of her family had she lost? Whoever she was, she didn't get out of the car. She was there when we exited the church, still smoking as if time had frozen her to the spot, but it gave me something to think about other than faking sadness.

***

David's mum is swallowing sausage-rolls. I'm sure she's scoffing them down whole. I can't stand the way she eats, how her jowls quiver when she chomps. There's a vulgarity to her that even David despised. Her own son found her despicable. Once, we spent a half an hour sitting on our door mat, hiding like a pair of kids, as she knocked and squawked through the letterbox, demanding we let her in. We didn't. We rarely did.

All I can think about is the woman with blonde streaked hair in a tight-fitting red dress that is perched on the edge of my cream sofa. She has mud on the tail end of her black coat, and if she turns even a fraction more, my sofa will be smeared. Why is she wearing red? What an odd colour to wear to a funeral. How did she know David? On closer inspection, I see it's Aunty Sue, his mother's, the cockerel's, sister. Of course, it is. She's lost weight, she looks great. Should I tell her about the mud or quickly shove a cushion under her backside? What would David do? He'd make a joke of it, but I'm no good at telling jokes or really understanding them.

Shit, she's coming over with David's mum. I'm about to be ambushed by the bitchy sisters. Best I should drink more wine.

"There you are darling. How are you holding up?" Aunty Sue says, brushing crumbs from the bosom of her jacket onto my cream carpet. My eyes fix firmly to the floor in horror.

"She's just fine. Look at her, not a tear for my poor boy, not a sodding tear. Cold-hearted bitch." She eats another sausage roll and washes it down with a gulp of wine.

"He should have told you. I don't know why he protected you so. What did you ever give him, eh?"

"Margery, stop it. It's neither the time nor the place." Margery stumbles back and catches her heels in the depths of my carpet, which I notice is full of shoe indents. Aunty Sue expertly takes away her glass of wine and only just manages to steady her by the elbow.

I wonder what she means about protecting me, but instead, put her comments down to too much wine and grief. For all of her bitter nonsense, I believe she loved her son.

I wish she had fallen, though, right onto her doughy face. Is that terrible? Margery's coral glossy lips are moving and smacking together like wet slugs, but I can't hear her words because I've decided to block out anything venomous. Her chin is jutting as she spurts her poison. She's always reminded me of a chicken with that loose, wobbly bit waggling about under her chin and with her thatch of faded red hair which is backcombed, coiffured, and secured with enough hair pins to supply the local hairdressers. The way she struts with her giant torpedo bosoms out front, she could pass for an overweight cockerel.

I can barely look at the woman without wanting to slap her. The thought of such a pleasurable experience forces out a laugh. I absentmindedly run my fingertips over the scar above my left eye, as I always do when having a wicked thought.

"See, cold bloody cow she is!" Margery spits crumbs through the gaps in her teeth. Aunty Sue spins her around and gives her a little shove toward the buffet table, then turns to give me a quick eye roll.

"The woman's an abomination," David had said. "A poor excuse for a mother. She only ever turned up when she wanted something and I'm certain today will be no exception, but as always, I'll be polite for David's sake."

"Let's go into the garden and get some air." Lucinda comes to my aid and guides me toward the patio door, her warm palm seeping heat into my lower back.

"If you need any help, Rosie, with anything, please let me know," Aunty Sue says sourly as we pour into the garden and I breathe for the first time today.

"Help? No, we have everything under control. Don't we, Rosie?" Lucinda shouts back. The sound of her voice is like a wonderful hug. I pull my gaze up to meet her big chocolaty eyes and my small blue eyes smile back. Thank goodness for my childhood friend.

"What is that woman's problem? The day she buries her son and she still manages to act like a complete idiot. Why did she even come? She hardly ever came when he was alive. Stupid old witch." Lucinda snarls and offers me a welcome cigarette. I breathe satisfyingly deep. I pull smoke into my lungs and hurl my frustrations back up into the clear morning, wishing I were anywhere but here on this surreal day.

Bright and crisp as the morning might be, the cheery birdsong is painful; a melodic joy that doesn't fit such a sad day. There's a sickly feel to it like it isn't real, like I'm not really here. The dappled shade of a climbing yellow rose is the perfect place to hide and smoke like we used to as kids. "Thank you." My words are sincere and the first I've uttered all day.

"You know, you should come to mine and leave the vultures to it. I can run upstairs and pack you a bag if you like. Meet you at the car in ten minutes?" Nodding is all I can do. I don't seem to have the energy to form words or articulate my feelings. Only Lucinda knows me well enough to see I'm struggling with the day's emotional pull. To others, I come across as cold and unfeeling. She hands me the keys to her car and shoots upstairs. Ditching my perfunctory black stilettos, I tiptoe around the side of the house, hugging the wall and ducking under the bay window, sucking on the last of my cigarette. David's work colleague Ewan is perched on the window ledge. He spots me and looks down to where I'm crouching. He presses a finger to his lips and gives me a sympathetic look. I show him a little wave as I shimmy in-between the cars and slide into Lucinda's passenger seat. Relief washes through me. I feel like I've just escaped from prison.

We saunter along the coastal road toward the Gower Peninsula. The sun dazzles and the water shimmers and the flickering draws my eyes to the volume of glittery sea. The day seems too beautiful to be in mourning. I glance at the wing mirror as a fleeting flash of blue catches my eye. The car parked at the church is behind us. I pull the rear-view mirror toward me in the hope that I can see the driver's face more clearly. But the woman driving is wearing a floppy sun hat and large sunglasses. She notices me looking because she hangs back and swerves off down a lane leading to a derelict farm.

"There was a car just now behind us. It was parked outside the church as well. There was a woman sat inside, did you see it?" I watch the roof of the car disappear along under the hedgerows as it follows the lane.

"Probably a coincidence hon. You just relax and enjoy the views."

"The car turned off down the lane to Henfryn Farm." Lucinda looks over at the farm and slides her glasses up over her head.

"That old wrecks' been abandoned for years. She's probably walking her dog along the old track behind it." Something about the car and the woman makes me shudder, but I focus on the gentle movement of the sea and begin asking myself questions - always questions.

Lucinda's hand is warm. She places it on my knee and we are comfortably silent, winding around country lanes while I lose myself in solitary thought. The shrill of her mobile phone takes me back to a day only two-weeks before, when things seemed pretty damned perfect.

TWO ~ Remember, Remember

"Can you get the phone, Rosie? And did you pack my white sport socks?" David says. And I wonder why he is playing sport on a business trip. He doesn't usually. The phone stops as soon as I pick it up.

"Why yes sir. I did so and your ugliest underwear too," I jest. Yet I have a theory that if he should meet anyone, he would be too embarrassed to get undressed to reveal Top-Cat or Scooby-Doo underpants.

"Still don't trust me after all these years?" I smile right at him and search his eyes for the joke. I struggle to read emotion from words alone.

"Of course, silly. Just having a bit of fun. Don't be such a grouch." I don't trust him and have lived in perpetual fear that he might meet someone else who can bear him children.

I watch him like a hawk as he packs a bag with his watch, laptop and wash bag which he fills with newly purchased expensive aftershave. He doesn't usually take it. I say nothing and keep watching as he rifles through his bedside drawer for his charger lead. He slips hand cream into his wash bag too. He goes into the bathroom and I can't help but delve into his wash bag for a root around.

There's a foil pack inside with two blue diamond-shaped pills inside. It's Viagra. I throw them back in the bag and zip it up. Tears spring into my eyes so quickly that I don't have a chance to recover and wipe them away before David's back and sat at my side looking seriously worried.

"What's wrong? You look upset." He pushes slim fingers through dark hair peppered with grey. He smiles so his dimples show either side of wide lips, and the lines around his eyes bunch. I'm jealous at how handsome he gets with each passing year. Yet, at the same time I feel happy at how my love for him never fades, despite my madness.

"Just had a random thought about my Mum's funeral. That's all." I lie. I lie to him a lot, because the thought of losing him terrifies me.

"Shit, of course! It's the anniversary of her passing. Rosie I can't believe I forgot. Forgive me?" His shoulders hunch and his piercing blue, mischievous eyes crinkle in apology. There's nothing to forgive. *My mum isn't dead.* Not in a conventional sense. She's alive and living in Scotland in care. They can never meet because my cover would be blown, and I like our life. He thinks I'm normal and I'd like to keep it that way.

"Sure. It was a long time ago; now let's get you to the station, shall we?" I hear a light knock at the kitchen door before it opens and Lucinda's voice chirps up the stairs.

"You got time for a cuppa, Rosie, before I go into Llanelli Town? I've dropped the kids at me mam's and I've got a hair appointment with that gay guy Ritchie. I'll stick the kettle on. Come if you like? I'll tell you all about my new seasonal toy boy and get you a trim for when that handsome hubby of yours is home."

"Still here," David shouts. His laughter travels down to her, deep and loaded with good humour. I know she's blushing.

"Oops, thought you were in London this week, selling your soul?"

"Toy boy. Eh?" David winks at me.

"Stop it. You know I'm kidding." Lucinda laughs nervously.

"I'm off on my travels now. My darling wife is taking me to the station, hey Rose?" He smiles at me. I'm in no mood for smiles, but I manage a fake one which he doesn't notice. He never notices.

"Yes love, we better get off."

"I'll lift you there now if you like. It's on my way." Lucinda says. I'm so glad. I don't want to be in the car alone with him. I don't want to have that awkward conversation, because it will turn around to me being paranoid about his non-existent infidelity. Lucinda always manages to come to the rescue.

"Okay, I'll be there now, in a minute. Sure, you don't mind?" He zips his case up. The sound is loud, like a machine gun. I look into his eyes as he leans down and pecks me on the cheek. He picks up his suitcase and lugs it down the stairs.

"Rosie, coming for that trim? We could grab a coffee after at North Dock and take that mutt of yours for a walk on the beach." Lucinda gives me that look she used to when we were kids and she was trying to convince me that skiving off school was going to be fun, but we always got caught and put in detention.

"That mutt is a prince. Aren't you boy? You should go wifey, get all tarted-up for when your handsome husband's back," David says, patting our chocolate lab on the head and curling those beautiful wide lips into a smirk.

"Prick," I say.

Mowgli spins his tail and jumps about the kitchen as David slips on his inspector gadget overcoat and picks up his suitcase. The sight of him leaving, his large silhouette pinned against the door frame, morning sunlight pouring in behind him, makes me shiver and prompts me to remember something about my old life. The sombre sound of a man whistling starts in my head, deep in the back of my mind, but I block the sound out because I don't want to remember it.

"No, I'll come and meet you at the beach after. I've got a few errands to run," I lie.

"Suit yourself, lovely. I'll call you when I'm done."

The sound of the door thumping shut is welcome. The eerie silence that follows leaves traces of David's deodorant and Lucinda's Angel perfume lingering in the kitchen. It gives me time to think about why the hell David has Viagra in his bag. On the horizon a blazing sun is dissolving into dark hills beyond the port and the view is calming. I'm not good at confrontation, but I am good at deception and living with hurt etched into my bones. I'll talk to Lucinda at the beach to see what she makes of it. She's usually good at diplomacy and not jumping to the worst conclusion. She has always been a good mediator and confidant and will give me a myriad of scenarios to keep me from bad thoughts. Although, this might be a tricky one to resolve.

David and I are perceived as the perfect couple by all our friends. We are madly in love but founded our relationship with the spoken understanding that we would, one day, have a big crazy family and that we would have a busy household. However, after numerous painful tests, it was discovered I can't have children. So, I can't keep my promise.

This has caused me to be insanely paranoid about

David's every move and my reasoning of why he does the things he does. I'm often wrong, I have stopped reasoning. Hence this morning's silence about the blue pills. Talking to Lucinda about everything is my catalyst for remaining sane because her rationality is the best thing about her, that and her two fatherless blue-eyed daughters: Summer and Sky.

Lucinda comes running toward me holding a red scarf over her new hairdo. Squealing like a child as the wind lifts her coat and the seagulls' wheel and cry overhead. The sight of her raucous and animated like some cartoon character, makes me smile. She hasn't changed much since we were kids.

"Ice cream or coffee?" I shout through the wind.

"Ice cream, mint-choc-chip, if you're buying. We can take it across the beach."

Mowgli is off ahead and sniffing up sea-vomit. He's ploughed so far on he looks like a puppy in the distance, chasing his tail and snapping at the waves.

"I found Viagra in David's wash bag," I shout as she approaches to take her ice cream.

"Tell the whole beach why don't you? Are you two trying to spice things up?"

"No, we have a good sex life; he never has a problem, you know, getting it up."

"Then maybe he thinks he's not satisfying you? You know what men are like? They're paranoid about that kind of stuff."

"What if it's for someone else?"

She laughs as the wind blows auburn tendrils across her face and sand sticks to her lip gloss, making her grimace.

"Not an option. You know how much that man worships you. Stop thinking that way, now. I bet you any money the Viagra will turn up in your bedroom soon. You just wait and see." She wipes away the sand with her scarf and lets her hair trail behind her like kite tails. She has a knack of waving away my insecurities and putting my world the right way up. Small clouds are forming like a cluster of bruises, bringing a smile to my lips. I've always loved stormy days. We both shiver a little and link arms.

We are halfway over the beach when a large thick-set man comes jogging toward us, out of nowhere, with his black hoodie up over his head and large headphones over the top. He must be blind because he ploughs straight into me and knocks me flat onto my backside. But he doesn't stop to apologise. Or help me up. He just turns to give me an emotionless stare. His eyes are dark, mean, and unforgiving.

"Shit, what the hell was all that about?" Neither of us shouts after the man because we both understand there is something about that penetrating look that was intentional, silencing.

"No idea. Did you see his eyes?"

"Rosie, that was scary. What kind of man doesn't even say sorry? What a bloody buffoon." We both summon up nervous laughter, but the incident changed the mood of the day. Unease follows me around afterwards. For the rest of the week I'm shaken up because who runs into someone intentionally?

The day before David is due home, I'm cleaning the kitchen. I stop for a coffee break in the back garden at our bistro table for two, which is perfectly situated to soak up the morning sun. Distant waves are crashing. It's hot and beads of sweat have gathered across my forehead and shoulders. I know freckles will burst across my nose and David will tease me about them. The coffee is scented and strong and the birds are in full chorus in our cherry-blossom tree. Mowgli is sat at my feet, curled into a chocolate donut in his sunny spot. I begin to compile a list for the shops and decide on a fish-platter and a bottle of red for David's welcome home meal. I imagine it plated on our dining table. Wine glistening under candlelight, rustic bread roughly chopped into a basket next to my fresh lilies. The sun pouring in through open patio doors. Something I've always done is visualise what we are going to eat. I wonder what colour lilies he will bring me. Secretly, I'm hoping it's going to be maroon.

The house phone rings and cuts into my peaceful

morning. I don't want to get up to answer it. I ignore it, but then my mobile rings. I ignore that too, but it rings again, and Mowgli lifts his head as if to say: 'Would you get that, please?'

Abandoning my flip flops under the table, I go barefoot across the warm concrete and pad across the cool white kitchen tiles. When I pick up the phone....

"Rosie, it's Lucinda. Listen to me carefully, please. Whatever you do, don't turn on the radio, or the TV." I laugh and wonder what she's up to now. It's nearly my birthday. Has she gone and done something stupid?

"I'm not joking. Sit down and do not move. I'll be there as soon as I can. Promise me you will not move." Nausea is instant. I don't know why. There's a stir in the pit of my stomach. I fill a glass with water. My hands are shaking so much it spills onto the table.

"Lucy, what's happened?" I ask. Fearing the worst. Her voice is serious, something I don't hear often. My first thought is something's happened to one of the girls.

"Just don't move. Or speak to anyone. I'm on my way, okay?"

"Okay."

I sit at the table when the doorbell rings. There are two large shadows looming behind the frosted glass. The police.

Immediately, I hear a man whistling the tune '*Melancholia*' in the back of my mind but order the sound to stop. I open the door.

The tall policeman asks, "Are you Mrs. Morgan?"

I nod.

"Is there anywhere we can sit?"

His eyes stay locked onto mine. The next ten paces toward the sofa are the longest I have ever walked. I sit with my hands wringing one another and sweat forms on my upper lip. I desperately wish Lucinda was here.

"I'm sorry to inform you that your husband has been involved in a car accident. Your husband died at the scene." He delivers the news that easily. "There was nothing the services could do. I'm so very sorry."

I remember feeling sad for the big policeman who looked as though he were about to cry. The female police officer couldn't look at me at all and didn't say a word. Numbness overwhelmed me, made me lightheaded; Yet still, I was thinking rationally.

"Where was he?" For some reason it was important that he died on home-turf. He was a passionate and patriotic Welsh man. I hoped he made it back over the border from England.

"Edinburgh, Scotland." The words were a blow. He was on a business trip to London. That didn't make sense.

I remember little else of that conversation, apart from he had been burned so badly there wasn't a body left to identify, then Lucinda making a pot of tea, and lots of macabre, confusing silence. There were screams somewhere inside my head. I've not felt ready to cry, but then I don't believe he's dead. They must be wrong. The words echoed in my mind. I repeated them to myself over and over.

They are wrong. He can't have been in Scotland. Wrong, wrong, wrong.

THREE ~ Questions

Lucinda pushes open the patio doors to a blustery day on the beach. A flurry of wind flutters the white voile curtains. The motion of a volatile sea rocking back n forth brings me back into the mute sadness of now. I step barefoot onto the decking. I've never liked wearing shoes. The summer provides plenty of opportunity to get air around my toes. David used to tease that I should have been born in the wilds of Africa. I think of him and us and I have a knot of volcanic anger buried and bubbling deep inside.

So, he really is gone. The selfish bastard's dead and gone. He promised me a life of happiness. He promised me the world, but then I promised him children. I guess promises mean nothing, in the end. They're just words of good intention.'

"Hey petal, you ok? You look like you're lost somewhere." Lucinda passes me a coffee. Steam rises, bringing the welcome scent of caffeine. The sea is peaking in white crests. I focus my eyes on the tiny birds riding the waves. The rolling motion makes me feel slightly nauseous.

"I wish I was. That blue car is playing on my mind. Why would it have followed us? Who do you think that woman was?"

"You sure you're not just imagining it? You know grief plays out in different ways?"

"Don't use your psycho-babble on me. I'm not losing it Lucy. That car was there."

"I'm sorry. That was daft thing to say but try not to think about it too much. It could have just been a coincidence."

"I don't think its a coincidence, I just don't understand why David's car would have been up in Scotland? It's driving me nuts, especially after finding Viagra in his bag. What if he wasn't the man I thought he was? What if he had a woman that was his fancy bit?" I'm angry at a dead man who's left me with unanswered questions. I have a desperate urge to scrape my arm a little. To ease the tension.

"Now, you're being ridiculous. That man worshiped the ground you walk on."

"So why didn't he tell me?" Something is gnawing at my stomach. A wave of anxiety, a new uneasy feeling.

"I don't know sweetie, but we can try and get some answers. Have you tried talking to Ewan at the boat yard? Perhaps he knows why David was there?

Business plans often change, and they worked closely together. Maybe it was a last-minute thing."

"He always told me everything Lucy. I don't understand. Something's not right."

"Don't jump to conclusions. Let's go over to see Ewan."

The back lanes toward Cardigan are tree-lined and plentiful. Some taller, lofty trees meet to form fairy-tale arches. Dappled sunlight drops through the leaves. I pop my head out of the car window to sniff up the smells of late summer and drink in the surrounding views. To my right is a steep drop into a valley where a wide river sparkles. Surging swirls are dramatic and beautiful. How is it possible for my mind to be able to focus on such enigmatic views when it's also juggling sadness and painful curiosity? I wonder how I can think at all. The scenery reminds me of the same journey we took eight years ago, on a day just like this, when David showed me the yard and offices for the first time.

FOUR ~ David

2010.

"Why won't you tell me where we're going?" David grinned like a naughty schoolboy, bunching the muscles in his jaw.

"Because then it wouldn't be a surprise, would it?" He reached over and brushed my cheek with his finger and his eyes were filled with love. We passed Cenarth Falls and he pulled into the car park. We watched the water gushing and tumbling over the huge boulders. He squeezed my hand.

"It's beautiful," I said.

"I know." He got a picnic basket out of the boot and we sat on a bench and ate a feast fit for a king. After we'd finished eating, we were sipping on the last of the champagne. David presented me with a small tin with a picture of two magpies on it. I opened it to find a set of keys.

"What are these for?" I quizzed.

"You'll have to wait and see."

"So, this wasn't the surprise?"

"Nope." I was truly mystified and hadn't a clue what he was up to.

We drove all the way to Cardigan and pulled up at a run-down industrial estate close to the harbour.

"What are we doing here?"

"See that red door over there?" It was unmissable. It was tall like a farm door, big enough for machinery to fit through with a smaller door cut into it.

"Open it." He handed me the keys and stayed at the car, leaning on it as proud as punch. I walked toward the building and fiddled with the keys until I found the one that fit and clicked it open.Inside the echoey space was a recently painted sign propped on three drunken chairs.

"Morgan Enterprises." I squealed with delight. his dream, our dream a family business fixing up boats and selling them on. He came over and lifted me up and swirled me around.

"Happy?" he asked.

"Yes."

We kissed, and we kissed some more. If I close my, I can still hear the clatter of my heels echoing through that cavernous building as I looked in every corner, imagining our new world.

"What do you think Mrs. Morgan?" "Morgan and Sons, one day, eh?" He winked at me. It was the happiest day I can remember. Before the shocking news of my infertility a year to the day later.

***

The yard is now complete with three polished, shiny buildings and boats of all sizes that are littered all over. The sight's a sad reminder of us. All our hopes and dreams were pinned right here next to all this. My head is light. I have the urge to get back into the car, drive away, and not face the place.

"Come on. Let's go inside." Lucinda gently pulls on my elbow, showing me her shiny white teeth as she gives me a sympathetic smile. I take a deep breath and step through the door. I am greeted by Wendy the company secretary, who looks as if she's been crying.

"Oh, Rosie, we didn't know you were coming. We're all so sorry. It was such a shock to all of us." She talks quickly.

"To me too," I reply.

She looks at the floor momentarily and then asks awkwardly.

"Are you here to see Ewan?" I nod.

"He's out on a yacht that came in for restoration yesterday. Dock three."

Lucy stays to chat with Wendy who looks as if she is bursting to ask questions. I navigate my way through the boat graveyard, passing coiled ropes, rusting anchors, snapped keels, and broken masts. I see Ewan rubbing down the underside of *Sea Voyager,* a beautiful, gleaming-white yacht. Working in a chequered red and black shirt, his large frame is busy rubbing at a blanket of tiny barnacles.

"Ewan, can I have a word?" He jumps up and wipes big hands down the thigh of his overalls and hurries over. His embrace is strong. He squeezes me with all of his might. He smells of sweat and deodorant. It's the closest I've come to crying. His eyes are full of tears. He gently shakes his head to stop them from falling. He coughs them away.

"What a shitty business, eh Rosie?"

"It sure is."

"How are you coping? I know it's a stupid question, but...."

"Shit, Ewan, totally shit and confused. I wanted to ask you about David's business trip. He was supposed to be in London. Did you know anything about why he was in Scotland?" I see a shift in his demeanour. He steps back, scratches at his whiskers, and shakes his head before speaking.

"No, as far as we knew, he was meeting with the accountants and with a new client who was looking for a yacht. He didn't say anything about Scotland."

"You would tell me if you knew?"

"Rosie, what a question. Of course, I would. We've been friends a long time."

I know he is lying. He blushes on his neck when he's uncomfortable, and his neck is practically glowing. Something is wrong.

"Who's this new client? Perhaps I could talk to him or her and see if they said anything."

"I'm not sure. He didn't say and there's nothing in the files." A seagull's cry breaks the silence. I know in my gut he isn't saying something.

"Well, maybe Wendy knows something?" I query, knowing they usually discussed everything to do with the business. I presume this trip must have been a personal one. if Wendy is clueless.

"No, we've already been through it. Honestly, we're as miffed as you." That confirms he's lying. My anger rises until it explodes out of me.

"Ewan, for fuck sake, my husband was found burned to death in a car, in fucking Scotland. There were skid marks at the scene. His teeth were so smashed in. There were no teeth left to identify him with. So, someone else must have been there. What's going on?" My arms start to flail because nothing makes sense, to hit out at the sky gives me a way to release something. Anger? Frustration? Rage? I scream. The world stops spinning for a second.

"I swear. I don't know." He wraps big arms around me and holds tight, so I can't struggle to get free. The heady mix of sweat and deodorant feels mildly comforting. It's good to be held. When I relax, and my breathing slows, he lets me go.

"Why don't you ask Karen?"

"What would Karen know?"

"He was meeting with her a lot; maybe they were talking about something important?"

"David's always been close to his sister. It was probably just everyday stuff."

"They were meeting almost every day, Rose. He was gone from the office for hours. He said they had stuff to sort out, family stuff."

This was news to me, more secrets. Why didn't he tell me if there was something important to discuss concerning family?

It's obvious I'm not going to get any information from Ewan. As a partner in the business, however, I'm entitled to look around David's office. To see if there are any clues as to his recent activity. His desk is neat and tidy. Nothing is out of place. No papers, no pens, no laptop with a screen saver of his wife and pet dog at Barafundle Bay eating ice creams, just an empty desk, recently polished and uncharacteristically bear.

"We thought we should move his things. We thought it would be hard for you to see."

"Isn't that a decision I should make, Wendy?" She shifts her gaze to the drawers.

They are full of loose papers and old pens, tattered

files, and post-it notes with random scribbles. An old mobile phone is underneath the debris. I presume it's an old model, left after an upgrade. I turn it over and there's a sticker on the back with a love-heart saying, *"Daddy's bat phone."* I place it in my bag. Lucinda is standing at the door and looking around, wrapping her arms around herself as if she's cold. I rummage around and find the charger.

"Come on Rosie, let's get home, and cook something to eat. I've gotta get the girls from Mum's on the way back." She seems suddenly eager to get away.

We are about to leave; I turn to Ewan who is leaning on the doorframe looking shifty. I pull the phone out of my bag.

"Ewan, is this yours?" I show him the phone. He looks at it curiously, but I can see it isn't.

"No, I've never seen it before." His neck stays white. Lucinda's eyes grow wide.

"What is it? Do you recognise it?" Her face is blanched white.

"No. Shit, I just remembered I forgot to pick up Summer's swimming stuff. We have to get going so I can catch the shops or there'll be murders." She laughs and tugs my arm like an impatient child. I slip the phone back in my bag and a cold feeling washes through me. I feel like everyone's acting strange. But even worse, I feel my vague past seeping into my memory bank and I'm afraid. David kept my past away. He was my unintentional defence gate that stopped my past from flooding in. Who knows what will happen now he's gone.

FIVE ~ Reality

I had little desire for coming back to the house and returning to the silence. I felt a duty to at least try and see how it felt. Lucinda hated the idea.

"Stay with us Rosie. It's too soon. Let us look after you." She had the girls make me poached eggs on toast and spoil me with handmade cards. But to watch Lucinda's life continue, normally, with her girls so bright and cheery was painful no matter how sympathetic they all were.

***

There are letters on the doormat. David's slippers are next to mine. The hallway feels cold and shadowy. For a moment I can't go beyond the mat, as if I might be devoured by grief should I move. But I brace myself and make my first tentative step. *Hell, this is weird.* Feeling braver, I take long confident strides into the kitchen, which suddenly seems overwhelmingly big. *I'm okay.*

After clearing away old food and washing a mountain of pots left after the funeral, I switch the kettle on and throw all of David's mail in a drawer to deal with another day. I have an urge to open all the windows wide and let the morning in, but when I do, it makes no difference. There's no shaking the feeling of emptiness. The rancid smell of wilting lilies brings nausea to my stomach. I stuff them in a bin liner and chuck them out the back, vowing to never buy them again.

On my way up the stairs, I let my fingers glide along the cool wallpaper. I push open the bedroom door. My bed is unmade, as if we had just tumbled out of it. I wonder how long it will be before I no longer say "we" and start to be a widow. Can it be that I didn't know the man who shared my bed all these years? I would have bet my life that I knew him entirely. The bat phone is in my pocket. After tossing it on the bed, I just stare at it before charging it. I drink several coffees while waiting. I turn on every lamp to take away the gloomy light in our north-facing bedroom. Then I pull a blanket over my legs before turning on the phone. This makes me smile nervously because that's what I usually do when I'm about to watch a movie in bed. However, my situation is no movie. This feeling is just the worst kind of anticipation and fear. There's definitely fear. What am I going to find? Is this where my life turns into an even bigger lie?

The phone flickers to life and does a couple of

beeps. My stomach jumps about as if tadpoles are wriggling inside. The screen saver is a picture of a cat, a black cat in a top hat. There are no messages or numbers, no contacts. Just a missed call logged at 11:05 from the day he died. By which time he would have already been dead. The bite of disappointment at finding nothing concrete makes me want to smash the lamp at the wall. Instead, I steady myself.

I call the number back but there's no answer. I scribble down the number and leave the phone plugged into the charger on David's side of the bed. It's funny to have something of his that's foreign to me. The first clue to a puzzle I know I will have to solve. There is a feeling of mystery lingering around wherever I go, ever-present in my thoughts, a myriad of questions. Maybe the police can shed some light. They must be investigating his death, surely. There was no body, just charred remains. There were no teeth and skid marks were at the scene. It sounds like something out of a thriller movie. A set up, perhaps? I've heard nothing from them. I should call in.

I'm startled when the home phone rings. It takes a minute for the sound to register by which time it's stopped. I call the number back.

"Rosie, it's me, Karen."

"Hey." I can't think what to say because her grief will be equal to mine, if not worse because she's emotional, normal.

"How are you?"

"Good, considering." I feel guilty using the word good.

"Why did you disappear from the service? People were asking after you."

"I couldn't face it, Karen. It was all so quick, so surreal. Ewan said you and David were discussing something important before he went away."

"Yes, we were. It's a bit sensitive, but I think you should know. Can we meet up?" My stomach leaps again. I fear all words spoken from that point because I know they will lead to somewhere unfamiliar and possibly dark, making my husband a stranger to me.

"Yes, let's meet at the lake. I can't face being at the house. Say 2 o'clock tomorrow?"

"Okay, see you then. Take care, Rosie." Her voice trails off, sad and quiet. I have the desperate urge to tear every cupboard apart in search of another clue. There must be something that would be evidence, but I don't know what I'm looking for. Before I know it, I'm sitting amid a pile of clothes, suits and trousers with the pockets turned inside out and drawers, upturned and emptied. The bedroom looks like a crime scene. My efforts are fruitless. Nothing is out of the ordinary here, so I decide the office would be the best place to hide things, then the shed. There's nothing out of the ordinary there either.

I smoke a cigarette at the back of the house and open the garage doors to begin my rampage there. David's BMW gleams silver as sunlight pours onto the bonnet. I run into the kitchen to retrieve the keys. I sit in the driver's seat, smoking and letting the car fill with smoke and permeate the fabric. David would have hated it. He hated me smoking, so I hid it.

A four-leafed clover swings from the rear-view mirror, but I block out its romantic meaning. I feel around the visors, under the seats and under the mats, letting my fingers explore. Nothing. Then I search the boot. As I'm about to close it, I notice the corner of a plastic bag sticking out from behind the casing where the rear brake light is. I tug at it. The bag's full and heavy. I remove the back bracket and wires poke out. It comes loose easily, and the plastic bag comes free. I open it slowly and find a couple of syringes, a burned-teaspoon, rubber straps and a bag of white crystals. My heart stops. I sink to the floor. I feel the cool concrete so hard, cold, and life -affirming on my backside. My head's thudding. It's suddenly difficult to breathe. *Drugs, not my David?*

I crawl out of the door. I lay flat on my back on the grass verge, looking at the sky and lazy white clouds floating by. They begin closing in on me, becoming darker. The world becomes like a jumpy charcoal sketch. The whistling returns. Only this time, I can't stop it. It grows louder. The looming silhouette in the door frame is accompanied by a loud torturous, dripping noise. A heavy downpour somewhere outside of a window, behind the scary man's silhouette, is slapping rhythmically on concrete, as if a drainpipe is broken. Fear runs through me in spikes, as if poison is working its way through my entire body. Then comes a searing pain in my head. Then there is nothing but darkness. An all too familiar light shuts me down.

***

I wake up in my bed, with a glass of water at my side. I can hear muffled talking and children's chatter. The room's been tidied.

"Lucy, what..."

"Your neighbour Florence called. The nosey old bugger thought you were drunk, passed out on the grass." She laughs and snorts.

"Thank you, again. It seems you are always there. Are the kids with you?"

"Summer is here. Sky is at her Grans."

"What time is it?" My head hurts when I try to move. Lucy shoves a couple of pills in my hand and passes me the water.

"It's 10 a.m. You've been out of it all night. It must have been a bad one? Probably all the stress."

"Shit, I'm meeting Karen today at two, I need to get

ready."

"Karen? Why's that? I thought you two never got on."

"She's got something to tell me about David. Apparently, they were discussing something important before he left for London or Scotland, as it were." She looks at the floor before meeting my gaze. There is an unfamiliar look about her. I dismiss this because of my confused state of mind.

"Rosie, do you want to tell me about the drugs? Don't worry I threw the bag out."

"It's not mine. I found it in David's car, hidden in the boot. I'm starting to think he was involved in something really bad, Luce."

"You're sure it's not your past coming back? You know, it's understandable, tough times and all that." I shake my head in disbelief because she knows me better than anyone. The question stings.

"I was fourteen. I was drugged. For God's sake Lucy, how long have you known me?"

"Sorry, hon. I'm just checking. I know, silly old me. I didn't mean to offend you. You're my best friend. You know that don't you?" Nodding hurts my head, so I lay down. The pillow is so soft my head sinks right in. I'm so tired a huge yawn escapes.

"David would never take drugs. Wasn't the car new? Maybe the drugs were left by the previous owner?" I hadn't thought of that. I had jumped to the bad scenario first.

"Maybe," I say, but there is nagging doubt and I begin to drift off with this on my mind.

"Well, you sleep a bit more. Let the pills do their job. I'll set the alarm for one, give you time to shower." I think of Karen, so like her brother. I'm looking forward to seeing his face in hers but dreading the talk, dreading her forthrightness and her need for embraces and tears.

SIX ~ Karen

I arrive at the lake early so I can take time to prepare for the sticky conversation ahead and calm my mind as best I can. I find a spot on a bench where a couple of swans are craning their necks and then biting one another in a display of courtship at the water's edge. There's a pink hue to the day as the sun begins its descent into the hills. The late afternoon light is bouncing across the millpond illuminating ripples in pink and gold.

My head is still fuzzy, half-asleep. There's a nip in the air that makes me pull my coat tightly around my waist. I notice I've lost weight. I'm not eating, just toying with my food and pushing it around plate after plate. I have no appetite. I have no hunger. I have no enthusiasm, just a head full of nauseating speculation. The feeling that my life's about to plunge into darkness is so overwhelming sometimes it's hard to breathe. As if I'm living under a sinister shadow.

"Hiya." Karen's voice is gentle behind me, as if she doen't want to startle me. I turn to face her, and the wind leaves my sails as I look at the same dimples, the same wide smile and icy blue eyes. For a second, I can't articulate anything because it's like I'm looking at David. I've spent twelve years disliking this very face. She's a gorgeous sister who I've been jealous of because of their sibling closeness. The irony is I love that face today because it's half of him. She's so similar. I shed my first tear. A single tear, warm on my cheek. Karen observes my pain and moves in for a hug with water brimming in her eyes too. I step backwards and it's awkward for a millisecond.

"It's cold," she finally manages, while taking a pack of smokes out from her bag. She sits beside me and throws her head back to look up at passing clouds.

"Funny isn't it, how we look up to the sky when someone dies. Who's to say Heaven is up there anyway and not on bloody Mars?" Karen's smile is weak, her voice trailing to a whisper.

"Who's to say he's in Heaven at all?" I reply, but instantly regret my waspish tone.

"Let's get this talk over with. What do you have to tell me?" My stomach dances with trepidation, curdling and sickening because I know she will enjoy this.

"It's not what you think." She looks me dead in the eye.

"How do you know what I'm thinking?" I hold her gaze as long as I can stand to, but the reminder of him is too much.

"David confided in me because he knew this would destroy you." My stomach churns.

"Oh, God no. Who was she?" I stare at the mud on my shoes and choke back tears.

"An affair, no. What would make you think that? He bloody adored you."

"Drugs, then?"

"What are you talking about? Did you know my brother at all?" She looks annoyed and flares her nostrils to expel lines of blue smoke.

"For fuck sake, Karen, spit it out. I'm dying here."

"He had cancer, brain cancer, incurable." The words tumble out quietly in slow motion. The world turns upside down. As it comes the right way up, I spew on the grass and over my muddy shoes. I place my head between my knees and I just breathe, in through the nose and out through the mouth.

"I'm sorry. He was having treatment. That's why he's been going to London, so often." The shock is sudden and unexpected. I try to focus on her mouth. She continues to speak words inaudible to me and then she begins to cry, what seem like fake tears. I'm so angry with her. It takes all of my might not to hit her sobbing face.

"He was dying?" I say to myself, but she replies. I'm glad my words put a halt to her ugly cry face because it smacks of competitive smugness.

"Yes, the doctors gave him six months, a year ago. He told no one apart from me." She is crying again. The sobs become heavy, uncontrollable and I find myself patting her shoulder as if she were a dog and hating her for knowing his final secret, the grand finale of covert information. *So, the fucking bitch has the last laugh.* I hate that, at this moment, I despise her and love her.

"Did he have treatment up in Scotland?" I find a ray of hope in my question.

"No, not that I know of. Do you know why he was there, yet?" I shake my head, not finding words that would confirm I knew little about my husband. Making her victorious in her knowledge. It shows in her knowing smile, his smile. For a second, the sight of her is confusing.

"I don't understand. Why he didn't tell me? It doesn't make sense." The sun picks out golden gossamer threads in her red-gold hair. She stares straight ahead unbothered by my question.

"He was worried you would get all crazy. He didn't want to rake things up. You know, with your mum dying from cancer and all." I want to scream. Because of my lies, David denied me a truth that would have brought us more time. Time to be us. But I suppose that's fair, a lie for a lie. A feeling of doom swirls around my entire being and I curse my mother for ruining even this, my perfect life. Even though she abandoned me when I was small and is now in a nursing home with no memory of me, I blame her.

"Your mother. Did she know?" I ask Karen, picturing Margery playing the doting mother, desperately clucking and clawing back a bit of respect at the final hurdle.

"No, he only told me. I wanted to tell you. I tried to convince him to let me, but he wouldn't have any of it. He said that you wouldn't cope."

Of course, he would say that. I'd spun a deceptive yarn, so long, sad, and complicated about my made-up former life that he would have protected me from emotional turmoil at all cost. This thought brings a slither of comfort and a dollop of self-loathing at just how deceitful I've been. I must stay calm and get through this, so I can go to the top of a hill and scream out my frustrations. I must take back control.

"Before I go, did he ever talk to you about being on drugs?"

"He was having chemo, Rosie. Where's all this coming from? He only drank on special occasions. He was squeaky-clean, you know that. what's all this talk about drugs?"

"Nothing. it's nothing. Look, I have to go. I need to process this. It's big, Karen, and I can't believe you hid it from me." I can't tell her about the paraphernalia I found in the car. Instead, I decide to work this out with Lucy.

I wait until Karen's driven away and repeatedly slam my hands down on the steering wheel. The pain feels good, such a tonic. I don't stop massacring my hands until there's blood and possibly a broken little finger. Then the tears come like heavy rain, soaking my face. They flood until my head throbs and then I shut down, turn off my emotions and begin the drive home.

Passing through Burry Port town, I notice the estate agent has pretty purple balloons outside and think maybe, further down the line, selling up and moving on, closer to Lucinda, might be a good option. I also spot the blue car that was at the funeral parked outside. I pull into the end of the lane and casually walk up to the car and peep inside. There's a pair of women's sunglasses and a newspaper on the passenger seat.

I don't feel brave enough to go inside the estate agents. So, I pull my car in down the road to keep an eye on it. I'm desperate to know who the owner of the car might be and think back to the day of the funeral. I remember the string of hibiscus flowers hanging from the rear-view mirror, which confirms this is the same car. *Who are you?*

My head is already reeling from the day's devastating revelations and my hands now hurt. I know they will be bruised by the end of the day and I'll have to explain them to Lucinda. An hour goes by and several people come in and out of the shop, but no one comes to the car. Sitting and waiting is soothing and calming. It gives me time to think about the last few days.

I'm glad I managed to cry, but so disappointed that a man I loved didn't come to me with such important life-changing news. The realisation that my secret-keeping means I lost vital time with my husband makes me want to run into the sea to cleanse myself. Cleanse away my brutal past and that's just the part I remember. I know it's going to chase me forever.

An attractive thickset man in a navy-blue suit comes out. He looks young and familiar. He jumps into the car, which throws me because I was expecting a woman. He flashes the indicators and pulls out and I follow him. It's not until I see his dark eyes in the mirror, I recognise him. He is the man from the beach. He seems less threatening in a suit, but nonetheless, a shiver courses through me. For a second, I contemplate leaving it. Not sure this is a good idea, I call Lucinda.

"Lucy, I'm following the blue car from the funeral. The man who ran into me from the beach is driving it. Can you come to find me?"

"What? How? Be careful, Rosie. Take the registration number and we can find out who the keeper is and then come home. Don't follow him, Rosie. I have a bad feeling about this."

"I have to, I'm on the old Carmarthen road going towards Kidwelly. Can you come find me or not?"

"I'm at a party with Sky. You can be a stubborn cow sometimes, Rosie Morgan. Please turn around and come back. Meet me at mine later. We'll find out whose car it is. Just don't follow him, okay?"

I agree, but I'm too curious to leave this alone and too damned angry at all the secrecy and the shrouding mystery surrounding my life that I feel I need to take ownership of this situation. There's nothing to lose. I'm not afraid, so I grip the steering wheel, making me wince, and hang back and continue to follow.

The car speeds up and down narrow lanes with towering hedgerows and I start to feel claustrophobic. The sky overhead becomes grey and bleak. Rain spots the window screen with coin size splats. I feel boxed in and start to hyperventilate.

The network of lanes is so winding. I can't see in front of me. My heartbeat begins to race and sweat forms on my palms. My pulse, at the temple is softly tapping. I hear the water dripping again, outside a window. That looming silhouette is in the doorway to a small damp room. It moves a step forward. The whistling is so loud. I cover my ears and squeeze my eyes shut because it's getting louder, louder.

In a snapshot, I lose reality and I'm in two places,

then and now. I feel a tumultuous fusion of fear and shadowy hauntings lurch at me. The roof of the car is under me. The car does a death-defying somersault toward the hedge and the world outside spins and spins in dark greens and greys. I close my eyes once more as the screeching sound grows louder and the smell of a rich, acrid smoke fills my nostrils and the rattle of loose metal shakes my foundations. I tumble around and around like a flimsy shirt in a washing machine, a boneless rag doll. I'm vaguely aware I'm upside down as the car skids to a thump. I know I'm held in my seat by the seat belt alone. There's a pressure building inside my head. I see small spots of blood drip, drip, dripping. I shut down and succumb to the whistling of the big man and distant sad-sounding church bells. There's just impossibly soupy-thick blackness as he takes another step.

SEVEN ~ Insanity

A soft pulsating beep of machines on the ward and the shuffle of soft shoes, are the first noises I hear, a quiet chaos. My eyes are sticky, my throat is dry and my head is sore, as I lift it from the pillow and feel stars of pain bursting inside my head. Lucinda is at my bedside, looking tiny in comparison to a huge bloom of peonies, out of which pokes token, helium, get-well balloon with a trailing pink ribbon falling in lustrous coils.

Her smile is the type of smile that she has when worried. It is the same type of smile she wore when Summer broke her arm at Go Ape last spring and subsequently, all the way to the hospital. It is a grave smile showing the deepest concern.

“Who’s died?” I ask, perhaps inappropriately. But, she laughs anyway and then her face turns serious.

“You gave me a scare. What the hell were you playing at? You could have got yourself killed.”

“I’m sorry. I couldn’t help it.”

“Don't do that again, you silly bitch.”

“Charming!” To speak hurts my jaw, as if it's had a fist to it.

“You said you wouldn't follow him and I'm guessing you never even saw where he was going?”

“No, but I had to. I'm trying to make sense of a very odd situation. I know he works at Two Quays Estates now, so at least I can find out who he is and what he was up to. I have a feeling he’s something to do with David's death.”

“OK, but next time wait until I can help. You shouldn't even be driving, especially as the seizures have started again.”

“I know. But since I haven't had one in over ten years, let’s not be hasty about sharing that info with the DVLA.”

“Alright, but from now on you're coming back to mine and I'll do the driving. I could do with the company. The girls are driving me nuts and the school holidays are so bloody long. You can help provide some aunty entertainment.” She makes jazz hands either side of her head and it hurts to laugh.

I don't have the energy to protest, so I agree.

“Oh, and the condition of your recuperation, is a daily walk on the beach and a hearty meal so we can talk through what's going on and fatten you up a bit. You're starting to look twiggy, okay?”

“Karen said David was dying from brain cancer.” I

spurt it out fast and the sentence sounds ridiculous.

"Fuck off." Lucinda's knee-jerk reaction is genuinely puzzling, but rather comical.

"I'm serious. He'd been paying privately for specialist treatment in London."

"No way. We would have known. That's impossible. Wouldn't his hair have fallen out or something? He seemed so fit and healthy."

"Well, she seemed pretty convincing to me. I can't get into my head that he wouldn't have told me though."

"That is very strange. You poor thing, that news must have really hurt."

"It did, but I'm also curious as to why. Karen said that it was because he thought I wouldn't cope, which doesn't ring true. I'm wondering if she convinced him not to tell me in a final act of spite."

"I wouldn't put it past her. Do you remember why you crashed? What happened just before."

"I remember feeling light-headed and everything going dark. As you said, it's probably the stress triggering it all again." I didn't mention the reoccurring whistling or the silhouette because she would have me hauled in for a psychiatric assessment and I'd had enough of those back in the day.

"In that case, we need to do a few stressless things; yoga, mindfulness stuff. I'll do a healthy shop."

"Lucinda, if you even think about making me wear

lycra and making me drink green-puke, the deal's off."

"Jogging, then?"

"Mm, we'll see. Will you do me a favour and do some investigating with The Care Trust. I want to verify that he was having treatment. I need concrete evidence to find out if Scotland played a part in David's treatment. It's the only thing that would make any sense. I'm thinking he might have had therapy there."

***

The fact that Lucinda is here, still picking up my broken pieces after all these years, feels tremendously warming. She ferrets around in her bag and brings out an old photo of us wearing dungarees. We must have been about fourteen, which would have been two years after my arrival in Wales. We are sitting on a farm gate in Porthcawl on a school trip. Her hair is wild, and her nose scorched from the sun. I'm hanging off her arm, skinny and dark-eyed, blowing a gigantic pink bubble. We look happy, untouched, and carefree. I think how even then I was good at putting on a good game-face.

"Where on earth did you dig that up from?"

"How about a trip there when you're feeling a bit better? We could do with a break."

"That would be great." The thought of eating bubble-gum ice cream and collecting unusual pebbles from the beach we played on as children, brings me a kind of reticent joy. The thought of being anywhere away from home is a welcome relief. Especially getting away from the boatyard where we'd built our dreams. That place is more difficult to be at than any other.

As I begin to doze from whatever calming medication is fed to me through my drip, I remember the whistling again and the looming silhouette in a door frame, just before the crash. Even weirder, I remember the smell associated with the memory, a damp musty smell, the pungency of it exploding in my nostrils. Worse, I remember the feeling of sheer terror as a heavy door clicks to and echoey steps move forward. The vision is so strong that I take a deep breath and want to sit up, but the sedation begins to work. Beyond that recollection, there's little clarity to these blood-curdling visions. I'm almost too scared to remember more and wish the flashbacks would stop now, because I'm positive that whatever dark story is lurking in my repressed subconscious, will change things forever.

EIGHT ~ Doubts

The girls are doing back flips and contorting into crabs and are generally bending about on the pristine daisy-littered lawn. Their wiry bodies coloured gold by a succession of midday suns, their faces bright red from exertion. They're tangling themselves in ways I only wish I could. The similarities to Lucinda and how she was as a child are remarkable, even down to the muscular arms and tease-worthy bum-chins.

I wonder if there is anything of their father about them. He is an absentee in their life, but they never seem to have missed out. I admire that Lucy has let me share them and be a part of their lives, even down to their traumatic births. I like to think I filled some kind of parental void. Summer reminds me of her mum. Her wild, uncontrollable, strawberry-blonde hair and mass of freckles, she's just as striking. The same high cheekbones and small mouth are just as lovely. She has her mum's playfulness, whereas Sky is serious, more pensive, but cracks witty one-liners that make you laugh out loud. This is a quality I love about this odd, small-framed, golden-haired child.

Neither girls have spoken to me about David's death, but both show their grief with small gestures; giving me an impromptu hug or stroking my hair and looking at me gently, softly. There has been an abundance of cute handmade cards with only sunny pictures. To see them playing outdoors and to listen their giggles tinkling around the garden is a wonder to behold. The normality of it brings a warmth that ripples through every cell in my body and soothes my soul.

David was a big part of their lives too. We were both involved, and both loved them tremendously. Lucinda had been incredibly generous with them and we'd watched them evolve from babies, to toddlers, to now. I mustn't forget the impact on them. After all, I know what it's like to lose a father at a young age and although he wasn't their dad, he was possibly the closest they had to one.

There were times, initially, when David would warn me about getting so close. He would even become agitated and tell me to stay away. But he started to love them too. Before we knew it, we were in deep. It was a strange triad of parenting to outsiders, but we worked, somehow. A new-age family, the benefits to the girls have been monumental. Both emotionally and financially. They have flourished into confident little ladies. I hope this detrimental blow doesn't affect their spiritual growth. I hope it doesn't do to them what it did to me because being a fractured human being makes living a normal life impossibly difficult.

There are questions I have about David's death that will badger my mind. Ewan knows something, I'm sure. As for Karen, her spite, well, there's something to be dealt with there too. There's nothing to lose. David isn't here anymore to halt me from having it out with his perfect little sister. He was protective of her because of their rotten upbringing with a single parent that didn’t want to be a parent, at all. She hated me from the moment she saw me, hated his attentions being elsewhere, and she put a barrier between us that was too high and too sturdy to knock down. So, in the end, I stopped trying, stopped wanting to because of her malignant hatred for me. It only contributed to my own deep-rooted self-loathing that comes from a past I can only remember in frustratingly small-time frames, as if I’m watching an old movie with no chronology.

Little memories come at will and give me a glimpse into a world that’s possibly best left in the past.

I look at the girls sparkle with happiness and admire how their lives are. I find it impossible to compare to whatever it was I had at their age. Was it a life? I’m not sure. I was alive for sure, but as a young girl I found myself surviving foster home after foster home until I came to Wales and found the foundations of a new life at the age of twelve. When I was eleven, I was told my mum was in a residential home because she had tried to commit suicide and after had some form of dementia. I had never told anyone, not even Lucy. I said she was dead.

NINE ~ 1996 East Midlands

I arrived at my first foster home at seven years old. This is my earliest recollection of life in general. I had three items with me. A faded photograph of my mum, whose opaque eyes made her look as if she were dead. Similar to one of those creepy Victorian portraits they used to take of the deceased. A doll that was so torn and tattered, it looked more like a shredded blanket and the clothes I stood in, which, as I recall, didn't smell so great.

I was handled like a piece of rotten meat by foster mother number one, who pinched her nose as she shoved me toward the bathroom, where she stripped me bare and forced me into a bath filled with cold water. I'd never had a bath before and smiled with delight, thinking I'd stepped straight into heaven. I squealed excitedly at the feel of it.

"Don't speak, Rosie. Be still and you'll be just fine." Her voice was deep, as a man like. I wondered why sitting still would make things fine. She gripped my upper arms with her witchy fingers to let me know she meant every word.

The water glistened and swirled as I moved. I'd let the water run through my fingers. It didn't bother me that a serious-looking foster mother scrubbed me with the back end of a washing up sponge, the abrasive dark green scourer bit, and medical-smelling soap. She washed my hair roughly, scrubbing and kneading my scalp with her fingernails, so rigorously, I thought my head might fall off.

The harder she scrubbed, the more I smiled. The more I smiled, the harder she rubbed. It hurt and tickled at the same time. The bath water resembled a muddy river. She just stared at me, a stern penetrating look, and did a lot of sighing while pursing her red lips on a stinky cigarette. It took a couple of baths to get me clean, but it felt good. I smelled like meadow-flowers once she'd doused me with talcum powder all over my puny body and roughly tugged a white linen nightie over my head.

Her name was Antoinette and she resembled an old hag from a fairy-tale. She was as tall as a door frame and almost as thin as a broom handle. Her body was crooked, as if she'd been snapped in several places and glued back together all wrong. Her limbs and joints poked out at unusual angles. Her hair was thick, wiry, and charcoal-grey. She wore it in a bun, which was pulled so tight at the temple, it slanted her dark-blue eyes and made her cheekbones look sharp enough to slice should you ever dare to get close. Her lips were so lined from smoking that her lipstick bled into the surrounding skin. She wore a fitted black lace dress every day.

At first, I had no expectations. I didn't know what to expect from people, or even how I was supposed to react in return. I just knew it was better than wherever I'd come from, which I'd completely blocked out from the moment I left. This had mystified even the best psychiatrists, baffled counsellors, and rattled the cages of hypnotists, who tried relentlessly to regress me to that place, wherever it might be.

I became an enigma. The social care system tried everything to get me talk about my past. Including the use of drugs to encourage me to go back to those days and remember them. Because the corrupt system and time period allowed it. The professionals refused to believe that I truly remembered nothing, apart from my mother's face, but it's true and to this day, I still don't remember. They gave up trying eventually. I was filtered through the foster care system and lost, shipped from pillar to post, as all of the ill-matched caregivers found me too much to handle. I arrived at Moel Llys Children's Home in Ammanford and it was there, I stumbled on the good fortune of my only real friend, Lucinda. From then on, everything changed.

TEN ~ Finding out

"After breakfast, we should go and talk to that man at Two Quays. It's time we find out what's going on."

"You sure you're up to it. It's only been a couple of days. what if he's aggressive?" Lucinda looks apprehensive and furrows her brow

"It's been two days too long. If I don't get some answers, I'm going to crack up. I doubt he'll be aggressive at his place of work."

"Drink up and get showered. I'll drop the kids at me mam's and we can drive on over." She pushes a smoothie in my direction and pulls a funny face.

"Do I have to?" I look at the smoothie, which is the colour of mud and turn my nose up.

"Drink!"

"Aunty Rose, can you take us to swimming with Mammy later?" Summer's big blue eyes bore into mine, making it impossible to refuse.

"I can, if you promise to be the best and win all the races." Her smile is as wide as a frogs and she hugs my leg.

I let the shower water run down my back in rivulets of warm and hot, my palms flat on the white tiles. The sound of the water is ferocious. Lately, my hearing seems to be super sensitive, especially around water. The sound of it seems to be amplified. I never liked standing next to a gushing river, or a rough sea. It always frightens me, as if it was going to pull me in, engulf me and drag me to the depths, but I've never known why. For a second, I see the shadow of a crow, or a dark bird on a window ledge in my mind's eye, but it flies away as I try and focus. Then, I see a flash of material, white with primroses all over. It twirls like the hem of a skirt and then it vanishes too. I turn off the shower and sit on the edge of the bath, suddenly worried that these visions are coming too quickly.

***

The Summer heat seems to have been vacuumed right out of the day, leaving a pre-storm chill. The sky fills with dark blues and purples like something out of a horror movie, making me question the decision to go on our private investigative quest. The drive to Two Quays is silent. By the squint of Lucinda's eyes, I can tell she has an uneasy feeling and doubts if we should be tackling this ourselves. She's humming to David Bowie's *China Girl* on the radio. She used to hum this way before school exams, indicating she's nervous, now.

"You're humming."

"And you're annoying."

"Fair enough. Look, if you don't want to come, I can go alone."

"And if you have another blackout?"

"I think I should go in and pretend to be looking for a rental."

"What if he recognizes you? "

"I was wearing a scarf. I doubt it. It was you he was intent on hurting anyway."

She parks several meters down the road and hangs around by the car door as she gets out brushing the creases out of her skirt and straightening herself out. Pulling her shoulders back, she marches across the road, lustrous red hair swishing behind.

"Don't be too long though, or I'll be having kittens," I shout after her.

"I'll try. Why don't you walk to the shops and get us a sandwich for after to pass the time?" The last thing I feel like is food, but I agree, even though I have no intention of buying any food.

I don't have to wait long. She's back at the car within a few minutes and a wave of nausea passes through me. I look behind her to see if maybe he's coming. Her face is more relaxed than when she left, so I presume it went well.

"That was quick, he wasn't there?"

"I asked the girl at reception who the car belonged to and she said it was the owner's Anna Jones."

"Was she there?"

"Yes, she's middle-aged, blonde, quite a cougar, classy looking, bobbed hair, smart type and suited up."

"Shit, what now?"

"Now, you go in and have it out with her."

"What if he comes back?"

"I'll text you if I see him. I'll be here waiting. Go on before you bottle it."

My legs buckle slightly as I push the door open and look around. My mouth's dry and metallic tasting. My eyes go straight to the woman in the corner, flicking through papers on her desk. She peeps up at me over her glasses, takes them off, and gently places them on the desk with well-manicured hands and delicate fingers. There's instant recognition, maybe even fear. Her eyes are wide. She continues to look me dead in the eye as I approach and then, she suddenly breaks into a fraudulent smile.

"Rosie Morgan, it was a matter of time, I suppose." She says my name as if it were mud.

Her voice is deep and soft, sexy, and something about her makes me shake with anger inside.

"It seems you have the advantage here; you know me. You are?"

"Anna Jones."

"Why were you at my husband's funeral?" My tone is sharpe.

"We're old school pals. Me and David go back a long way." I can see she must be a decade older, so that doesn't sound right.

"He never mentioned you." She doesn't reply but raises a condescending eyebrow.

"Last week there was a blonde man driving your car. Who is he?" She looks surprised at my question.

"My son. Why? Is there a problem?" Her look changes to genuine concern.

"There was an incident at the beach just after David's funeral. Your son knocked me clear off my feet, intentionally, and I want to know why."

"I think you must be mistaken. Maybe it was an accident. Tom wouldn't do that. He's a good boy."

"It wasn't a mistake, or an accident." My answer is quick; she looks flustered and flicks more papers around, avoiding eye contact.

"I have no idea what you are talking about. Why don't you ask him? He's at home today, up at the campsite. Here's the address." I'm surprised she gives it so willingly.

"Were you and David…?" She laughs and tucks her neat bob behind small ears.

"No, nothing like that. He's a good guy. Look, we are part of an old group of friends. Let's say acquaintances. We share a similar history. I was at the funeral to represent those people." Her eyes are lying.

"He never talked about any acquaintances."

"He wouldn't. That's how they prefer it."

I feel very queasy. Her words seem to stay in my head and multiply into a million questions while she stares at me with sarcasm in her eyes. I want to ask her who these people are. Why didn't she come inside at the funeral service? Who is she, really? I summon the courage.

"Why were you following me after the funeral?" She purses her lips and pats her forehead with the back of her palm.

"I wasn't aware I was. It must have been a coincidence."

If there's one thing I do know, it's that coincidences don't exist. Probability, yes, mathematical and scientific explanations, yes; coincidence, no.

"Is there anything else I can help you with? I have to get on." There's a trace of irritation to her voice, but she smiles politely.

"No, that's it." I can't think straight, and my tongue feels big in my mouth. The room spins as I turn to leave.She adds "Oh, by the way, sorry for your loss. David was a good man. If you do go up to the campsite, mind the dogs. They can be vicious little shits, tear your fingers off if they got a chance."

The atmosphere changes in that last syllable. Her smile is suddenly wicked, pure evil, and I can't wait to get back to the car to let out hot tears of frustration. More lies, more unanswered questions, and more to seek out. By the time I arrive at the car, Lucinda is out sat on the bonnet, puffing on a fag. I fall into her arms and let it all out.

"Bloody hell. It wasn't an affair, was it?" Her concern makes me laugh.

I explain the conversation. She suggests we go home and investigate online and if we don't find anything, she has a friend in the police services who owes her a favour. I feel compelled to get to the bottom of this but start to feel exhausted, and tell her to drive us home, so I can rest and mull around the new conspicuous findings. Somewhere, in the back of my mind, as we drive alongside the sea I hear *'Oranges and Lemons'* quite randomly, a song from a time that I've lost. The chant of it makes me cry silent tears, for a reason I don't know yet, but I think it's coming for me.

***

Lucinda is called in to the hospital to psycho-analyse a young male, after his fifth attempt at suicide. I'm alone, bored and trying desperately to unravel the events of recent days. An internet search on Tom Jones only brings up posts and articles about the famous singer. The ransacking of our marital home for clues of a possible 'other life' also proves fruitless, so the only option is to visit this Tom, to find out who he is, what he wants and why he targeted me that day. I'm beyond fearing anything. Today, I just want answers. Going alone means getting a roasting from Lucinda, but then, she's been giving them to me all her life.

I reach a power-blue and cream sign for '*Sea View Campsite'* up on the crest of a hill with panoramic views of The Mumbles. It's small and caravans and campers are placed in neat lines, tiered, looking over the bay. It's well maintained. The grass has recently been cut; the smell strong, earthy. At the bottom of a fox- glove lined drive, behind the reception cabin, is a small stone bungalow and attached to it is a granny-annex. It could be a period property with ivy smothering one side like a creepy, masquerade mask.

I park in the semi-circle lay by and walk over to reception, where a young woman is behind the desk tapping at her phone screen with fingernails.

"I'm looking for Tom, is he about?"

"He's up at the house, seeing to Ninny." She doesn't look up from her phone but pops a large bubble with her bubble gum and laughs. I presume Ninny to be an animal.

"You want me to call him?"

"No, it's okay. I'll take a walk up." She still doesn't bother to look up.

The front door is blocked off with boxes inside a porch. I walk around to the back and through a small archway, leading to a walled-garden and a pristine lawn with neat borders, filled with fiery-red snapdragons. It's a stunning garden with a simple water feature at the centre, a circle of stone. The clever use of only red flowers is quite breath-taking against the vivid leafy greens.

The back door is open ajar, and my heart starts to drum, my breathing quickens. For a second, I contemplate leaving, quietly. I stand in the doorway holding onto the frame to steady myself.

"Hello, can I help you?" His voice startles me, and I jump around to face him. The eyes of a blackened soul stare right at me from the shadowy stone archway and my blood runs cold. I've never seen eyes so naturally dark, almost black. He recognizes me and then, his eyes seem to soften to murky brown. He's bigger than I remember and in casual clothes, track suit bottoms and a pristine, white vest.

"What are you doing here?" I can't figure out if he's a danger or not as he walks toward me with an empty mug and bowl in his hands, hanging loosely at his sides, as if he doesn't know what to do with them.

"You shouldn't be here. You should leave, now." I can't fathom out his look. I think he looks worried, even scared, and glances behind him, over a robust shoulder.

"Why were you at the beach that day Tom? I know you knocked me down on purpose." His eyes fill with what seems like embarrassment and I feel brave.

"You were in the wrong place at the wrong time." More lies.

"No, you don't get to make excuses. What is going on? I need answers."

"It's not up to me to say. Please, you should go. It's not safe for you to be here."

"Safe, why Tom? Why is it not safe?"

"Because if he finds out, he'll hurt you."

"Who Tom? Who will hurt me?" My voice is loud, and he lurches forward and covers my mouth. I try and muffle a scream, but he's too strong. He drags me backwards onto the house and sits me on a chair, roughly, so it rocks with my weight. Once I'm still, he lets me be and I shake so much the chair rattles.

"Look, Rosie, you need to stay away from here. It's not a safe place. I can't say any more than that." He speaks quietly as if he's trying to avoid getting someone's attention. In that moment, I realise it's not him that is a threat. Tom is afraid of whoever he doesn't want to hear us.

"Okay, I'll leave, but you call me if you feel able to talk. Here's my number." I leave my business card on the table and get up to leave feeling confident he will, but still shaking.

“I didn’t mean to hurt you that day, just to scare you.” He looks ashamed.

“You did that alright.” I make my way to the door and once safely inside the car, I breathe.

I have no intention of leaving without answers, so I drive down the lane and park under a row of trees where the car's hidden by dense foliage.

I make my way back up a steep hill on foot toward the rear of the granny annex. There is an abandoned greenhouse lodged at the bottom with a pane of glass broken on the roof and a slab path zigzagging to the back door. There is no grandeur in this place, a basic chalet with no frills. Whoever lives here isn’t green-fingered. The place is unkempt, weeds sprouting from cracks and brittle plastic, plant pots littering the overgrown garden. Green mould is staining the pebble-dashed walls in long streaks from a broken drainpipe.

I hear movement inside, the rattle of pots in the kitchen. Then I see a small old man stooped and balding, shuffling from the sink to the fridge. He looks up and lets his eyes rest on the decaying garden and just stares. My breath suddenly escapes in a gasp before I can stop it. It’s David. Older and more, but it’s him alright. The same deep dimples, the piercing blue eyes, the angular shape of his face. It’s all a replica of my dead husband. I drop onto an old crate, weary with disbelief and observe as the old man shuffles about doing this and that. There's no denying this man is somehow related to my husband. The resemblance is too uncanny, perhaps even the father he never knew. The father he told me died when he was a small boy. He said that's why his mother hated me so because their bond was tight, until I came along. If he was fatherless too, why wasn't she more understanding of my situation? That never made sense.

"She's a nobody, from nowhere, no family, no friends. What do you know really about that little orphan tramp, David? Stay away from her. She's trouble," his mum warned, as I stood in the kitchen doorway, mortified, listening, the first time I met her. She barely acknowledged me and that's when David began to hate her.

I make my way to the car, eager to get to Lucinda's to talk this through and gain some sort of perspective. The day just got bat-shit crazy and I know I need my old friends' guidance and comfort to see me through.

ELEVEN ~ Panic

Seeing my state of panic and hearing me gush out words that make no sense whatsoever, Lucinda runs me a bath, insisting, “Breathe. Relax first. Clear your mind and then we'll talk this mess through.”

For a moment, I think I detect mild irritation, but shake away the thought, thinking it more likely my constant state of paranoia is to blame. She folds towels on the edge of the bath, lights a cherry-scented candle, and quietly leaves me in a low-lit room with a flickering flame and a bath filled with warm, steaming water. I slip out of my clothes and submerge myself wholly, realizing this was a good idea after all. Being under the water is overwhelming, echoey and tranquil the world stays muted.

I roll a towel under my head and close my eyes, letting the water wash over me in swirls and hot surges as I move my hands. I imagine being a mermaid and flick my feet. My stomach tightens when warm water passes over it. The children are quiet. Lucinda has probably asked them to keep the noise down.

The tap starts to drip into the water. It's loud. I find the cacophony bothersome, almost torturous. A noise that brings with it a hint of fear. I feel as though I'm falling, like you do in a hopeless dream, but lately, it happens when I'm fully awake. A senseless sensation I can't relate to anything. It becomes vociferous and my bath time has turned into an unpleasant experience. Seconds later, I'm out and towel-drying my hair. I'm halfway down the stairs when Lucinda spots me.

"What is it with you? Are you allergic to water, or something? That's the quickest bath ever."

"I just can't relax. I'm freaking out about today, Lucy. My world is getting so bloody surreal. I don't know what the hell is real anymore."

"So, this old fella, you say he's the spit of David. You sure it's not just a similarity?"

"I'm positive. He was exactly the same, just older. You have to see it."

"And this Tom mentioned that some bloke might want to hurt you?"

"Yes, I can't get my head around it. Why would anyone want to hurt me?"

"Could it have something to do with your past?"

"If I could bloody well remember any of my past, then I'd have a clue. This is to do with David, Lucy, not me." I snap.

The situation suddenly feels overwhelming and I

burst into tears. Lucinda does her usual and pulls me into her while stroking my hair and telling me, "We'll sort this together. Don't go stressing. I'm sure there's a logical explanation for everything." Usually, her words take me to a place of reason and take away the panic, but I feel it lodged in my chest making it difficult to breathe.

Sitting at the island in her seaside-themed kitchen, my mind reels. I watch her chop, peel, and throw together an evening meal. She pours two large white wines. The instant sedation as it settles in my stomach is the most relaxed I've felt all day and I let myself stay in a place of calm awhile.

"If David was hiding stuff from you, I doubt it was sinister. He isn't the type. What if he was trying to protect you from something?"

"But we had no secrets. I don't understand. We talked all the time. Maybe he got into some kind of trouble. Maybe it was another woman. I think I need to go back up to the campsite and see who else is at the granny annex. Tom had been seeing to someone. The receptionist said it was Ninny. At first, I thought it was a dog, but he was holding an empty mug and bowl as if he'd fed someone."

"No way! It's too dangerous. You should talk to Anna, see if she will come clean. In the meantime, we need to go shopping. Mowgli's out of food and the kids need a few bits. You up for it? We can go to Cardigan in the morning and grab a coffee and cake after."

The distraction is welcome idea. I agree without hesitation.

We drive into the town and as we approach the car park. I catch sight of a familiar dark blue jacket. We park up. I see that it's Ewan, talking to a petite woman with bobbed blonde hair, wearing a knee-length blue summer dress. They are close, perhaps intimate, which is confirmed a moment later when they embrace and kiss tenderly. The woman turns to leave and hands Ewan a small brown envelope. She turns again, this time to face us, and Lucinda gasps.

"Isn't that…"

"What the hell? That's Anna!"

"Ewan's married. What's he playing at? Lucy, what's happening here?"

It's a peculiar feeling, my trepidation. It keeps me in a permanent state of fizziness, not knowing if my thoughts are sensible or irrational, real or not. My first instinct is to run after him and shout. He has a lovely wife. How could he do this to her? Then, I wonder if maybe there's a bigger, wider explanation they are all in on, a secret that I'm not yet privy to.We return to the house, get shit-faced on white wine, and go to sleep early after speculating that the world we are discovering is about to become explosive. I'm glad I'm not alone.

TWELVE ~ Dreams

I've not slept a wink, tossing, turning, and watching shadows move across my bedroom wall as the clock ticks away time. The darkest blue of night shifts to early morning peaches and golds and I'm glad for the normality of daylight.

My mind is still racing with so many questions. I fear I'm going to crack if I don't resolve at least a bit of this confusion. Who are these people up at the campsite? Why the bitterness toward me? I'm beginning to believe I'm linked to them all, somehow, but how? I reach over to turn on the bedside radio to stop myself thinking, block out my internal interrogation, all the time thinking, thinking, thinking.

Lucinda knocks the door and pushes it open with her foot, bringing a cup of tea some toast.

"You look how I feel." She smiles.

"Then you must feel like shit?" I whisper. She places the tea next to me and quietly leaves to see to the kids before school.

The buzz of my mobile makes me cover my delicate

ears. The caller number is withheld.

"Hello." My voice is hoarse.

"Let this be a warning. If you're not careful, you're next." The sound of the phone slamming on the other end is final, like a coffin lid shutting. I drop the phone onto the bed and freeze.

It rings again.

"Rosie, it's Karen. Mum's dead. You need to come quickly. I don't know what to do."

At first, the words flutter around in my head, but I come to my senses connecting the two phone calls. I leap out of bed and pull on jeans and an old t-shirt. Run out of the house without explaining to Lucinda, who is standing in the garden in her pjs looking worried, as I speed off in her car.

Karen's in the kitchen, sipping on tea, her face streaked with tears, her hair dishevelled, and she looks ghostly. Aunty Sue is pouring tea and is muttering to herself licking tears from her lips. The whole scene is extraordinarily surreal. My insides are shaking. We don't hug because it would be unnatural to both of us, but we rub arms.

"What happened?" I muster up sympathy.

"She locked herself in the garage, in her car, and turned on the engine after stuffing old socks in the exhaust. I know she was devastated about, but this is not something she would ever do." She cries hard and blows her nose into a snotty hanky; she looks a mess and struggles to find words.

This is my warning. Now I see the story unfolding is complex and should be left alone. *How can I?* It would be a lie to say I feel remorse for Margery's death, but I am sad for Karen. I'm also, at this moment, very scared.

***

Five weeks after David's funeral and I'm back outside the same old stone church, feeling sadder than I was then. This feels less formal. There are fewer people, less tears, yet for some reason, I'm swamped with grief and feel no need to hide my tears.

The service is quick. Karen is talking to the handful of mourners and I can tell she's on autopilot. She looks relaxed and lighthearted. She's making dull, false conversation, as she flutters from one person to the next attempting to smile. She'll melt when she gets home, a brother and mother gone and so close together. To those who feel, it must be agonizing.

To my disbelief, the blue car's back, under the oak tree, but it's neither Tom nor Anna in the driver's seat. It is the old man from the granny annex. David's doppelganger. He's looking directly at me, not the throng of people milling about. His look is intense, mean. It's strange, David's face so filled with malice and yet David's dead. To say I'm furious is an understatement. I march over to the car, suddenly filled with rage at this stranger's audacity. When I reach the kerb he purposely pulls away, screeching, sneering at me tauntingly. He leaves smoke in his wake. The small gathering of mourners are unimpressed. I'm intent on getting to the bottom if this. The control he has of the situation makes me mad and I wipe away hot tears but I'm determined to take ownership.

Days after the funeral, Karen and I are going through Margery's belongings, sorting out piles for the charity shop and boxing the more sentimental items for Karen to keep. It's strange how a life looks when it's sorted into piles. I find it therapeutic and a little tragic that we place so much value into stuff that ultimately goes into boxes or off to rubbish tips. I've been allocated the attic. It's a small stuffy space, everything is so layered with dust that even my lightest footsteps cause a flurry that choke me and make my skin crawl.

I open a circular window to let in some fresh air and begin to move things slowly to the side, ready to pass through the hatch to Karen, who's sifting through old papers. I shuffle box after box of old videos, magazine collections, all sorts of jumble that is of no importance to anyone but Margery, the dead cockerel. I kick a smaller box and it skids across the floor. I pick it up to wipe it free from dust and sneeze five times. It's a pretty cigar box, carved in walnut and ivory. It could be African. When I open the hinged lid, I'm surprised to find a bunch of yellowing letters and a couple of official-looking documents. I unfold the top one, slowly, so the dust doesn't find its way into my throat. I discover that it's adoption papers, dating back forty-years. I perch myself on a tall box, curious to find out more. I forage deeper, below the papers. I find a ring, a man's gold ring with a blue stone on the front that I believe to be a sapphire. It's initialled S. J on the inside and it's heavy. I skim through the writing on the adoption papers, hungry for information:

'*Baby Seth. Presumed to be six weeks old. Mother unknown. Father unknown. Origin of birth, also unknown.*'

Looking through the other documents, I find the baby was left at the edge of a woodland area, near a cottage and next to a footpath path in West Wales. Margery adopted the child on the 19th September. David's birthday. He was adopted. He can't have known. He would have told me, surely. Does Karen know? Is she adopted too? I feel faint. It's a delicate matter; I can't ask her out right.

The jolt of information is enough to make me hyperventilate. The room shrinks, dust fills my nostrils, and I can't breathe. I can't see further than arms-length. I try to stand, but trip over the boxes and land on my arse, having a full-blown panic attack. The world fades to black and the whistling begins.

At first, it's subtle, in the background, way off. Water drips, drops, taps onto moss-covered stone and the sound is so very loud. I'm cold, under a cloud, a threatening fog in which something lurks, yet there's sunshine pouring through the trees. The whistling sound is becoming enormous, terrifying. A bird flies into the sky until it becomes just a dot beneath a blazing sun. A flash of white material swirls and swooshes and fear is wedged in my throat, disabling my voice. I close my eyes and feel a strong hand around my upper arm, the grip's tight, unfriendly. I can't find my voice to scream. "Rosie, Rosie, are you alright? Did you fall." Karen has made her way up into the small space and is shouting, staring down at me while I'm clutching the letter. I scramble myself upright and claw my way out of the attic, still breathless and sweating. I tuck the letter inside my pocket and ask if she would mind me keeping the box as keepsake. She looks bemused but agrees. I make my excuses and go home to my empty, cold house. I sit on the doormat and sob into my hands for what seems like forever. When I'm done, I whisper,

"David, what's happening? Who are you?"

***

After a while contemplating and slurping down a mountain of coffee, I start to remember further back, to a time when I was so alone. I feel like this now, as if I'm retreating into my very small shell.

The Padgets fostered me for six months, when I was eight. They were foster home number two. The couple were so filled with love for a dead son, they had practically died inside. They despised the fact I wasn't him. They took their grief out on me. I was their emotional punch bag. I became a person to take their agonising screams out on. I witnessed them rain their frustrated blows on walls and doors. I saw her curled in a ball, him bone-soaked in booze and crying like a baby.

Their home was an old schoolhouse, left to decay, in an enclave at the back of beyond. It was a scarred husk, red brick. It had outrageously big rooms with acres of scratchy brown carpet. I rattled around in it, imagining it filled with children, imagining the hallways brimming with life. I could picture their dead son Christian in my head, running around in the rambling gardens, swinging from the now rotting tree swing. I can imagine him being admired from the kitchen window by doting parents. Grief is a funny animal, how it changes a person. I could see the couple had loved once, but that love became a deformity. It had pickled itself into a vinegary sourness that moved through their veins, the poison killing their kindness, and I took the brunt. They inflicted me with their pain. Luckily, I was used to it. I became hard as nails and chose to build a high defence, a solid wall that couldn't be knocked down. I couldn’t be broken, not by fists, or words, or even the truest form of malice. I was a paradox, an intricate puzzle. unbreakable. I learned to stay quiet and to say nothing.

"How dare you sleep in my boy's bed? How dare you touch his toys," Mrs. Paget would slur with alcohol scented whispers, after brandy had saturated her mind and contorted her bony face.

"I don't know why she wanted ya, a bloody girl. If it keeps 'er 'appy, then I s'pose you can stay, but stay outta my way, ya hear," Mr. Padget would say, quietly so his wife didn't hear, tapping a dirty fingernail at his nose.

I would blink my response, too afraid to talk because he had the meanest eyes I'd ever seen. and I'd seen a few by then. His hands were big, his fingers fat and swollen, the skin stretched around them like sausages about to spit in the pan. His face was ruddy. His nose was a network of small purple veins. His legs were the longest part of him and even they were stout.

When he was sloshed, he would sit me on his knee and touch my thigh in a way that felt wrong. I was sure that if I stayed there longer than I did, he would have let himself hurt me some more, touch me in a dirtier, scarier way. Thankfully, Mrs. Paget handed me back. She said that she couldn't cope with my quietness. I think she knew.

"The child gives me the creeps, how she just sits

there and don't talk. There's something not right about her," she told the social worker, who came to take me to foster home number three.

I remember all the small details: random pieces of antique furniture looking small in the gigantic rooms, with scratches all over them; smells of frying bacon in the mornings and booze tinged air at night. The couples voice tones were impatient and sharp, always sharp. That's what I don't understand about not remembering what happened before I went into the system, that sense of belonging to somewhere or someone. How could I not remember? I came from two people. Who were they?

***

Lucinda had a clever way of reeling me in, slowly, carefully, as if I were a fish trying to escape the hook. Once she'd secured me, lured me in with stories similar to my own, I let my guard down for the first time. I forgot to be a shoulder-pinched, curious, and suspicious little girl. I found the emotional attachment to another human being overwhelming, exciting. I grew up and exploded with confidence. It rained out of me like wedding confetti. That's what David says attracted him to me, my confidence.

"You're so bloody full of life, Rosie. I hope I can keep up with you," he said.

It was at school when I saw Lucinda for the first

time, fagging it behind the school bike shed. She looked uncomfortably cool, Gothic looking. Her hair was dyed jet-black, her eyes caked with smudged black eyeliner. She chewed on gum, trying to look cool and cocky. She was different in a way that smacked fake, a disguise to mask her vulnerability. I could tell behind the eyes she tried to make mean and her don't- mess-with-me attitude, there was a girl just like me, scared, broken. The first words she said to me as we left our English lesson were, “Didn't your mother tell you it's rude to stare?”

“My mother’s dead,” I told her, smugly. Knowing at the time that she wasn’t.

“My dad's dead too.” She tapped the cigarette packet so one popped out. She offered it to me. I thought it was the coolest thing I’d ever seen. That's how me, her, and David formed our little union, an alliance. All members of our group had one or both parents’ dead. A group of misfits, but we made it cool. We found strength in one another and rebelled against the norm. When Lucinda left for London in her mid-twenties to pursue her degree in psychology, we were devastated but we had one another. David and I married not long after. Thinking back to those days is my happy, sunny place. But still things are changing. They always change. I always knew deep down that this time would come.

THIRTEEN ~ Walking

It was decided, in that place before wakefulness, before my eyes opened and when dreams were still lingering in my mind, that I would set off for a long hike in the Brecon Beacons to clear my head and march out my accumulating stresses on those beautifully barren hills. My rambling across sheep-littered hillsides, feeling so small in that majestic place had often solved problems that at the time seemed monumental. I'm sensing my current problems aren't going to be so easily fixed. I long for this soothing solitude that I only seem to find at great heights or more recently, the bottom of a glass. With peat bogs, soggy marshes, and dried blonde grass underfoot, the sheer navigation of tricky ground while taking in panoramic views has a tranquil, calming effect and I desperately need to feel calm.

I need to feel the mountain breeze on my skin and the sun on my face. As much as I adore my dear friend Lucinda, her obsessive nurturing and comforting has become marginally suffocating. I'm still too afraid to return to my home because it feels haunted by a wonderful past, now lost. A little time out will allow me some much-needed thinking time, so I plan to sneak out, again.

Telling Lucinda how real this all just got would start a conversation I'm not ready for. Not yet. Recently, the creeping agitation I detect in her voice, I'm not sure whether it's real. I'm starting to hear discontent in everyone. My head is all over the place and I'm suspecting everyone around me of keeping secrets. My perception of life seems to be eternally muddled.

If she knew how shit scared I really am of the old man's cautionary and threatening voice that's out there, and that I feel him watching me, her panic and worry would increase my own. It would turn into terror and I believe that my flashbacks are taking me there anyway. So, I have to navigate this carefully, orchestrate my situation so I can handle my fear. The culmination of circumstances is already making me peek over my shoulder, jump at shadows, and avoid poorly lit places.

I contemplate being alone in the hills, whether it's safe, if I should be going, but I need the space. I desperately need it. I decide I should go because it's what I do when unsure about life, and what better time than now. I take Mowgli for safe measures, not that he's much of a guard dog. If there's one thing I was good at growing up, it was working things out for myself. Trusting no one and keeping my wits about me. Foster care saw to that.

The car's hot, swimmy. The air conditioning's been broken for six months. It was on David's to-do list. The four-leafed clover swings like a pendulum, ticking out my pain. I turn the car out of the drive with the windows fully down, Mowgli licks up the summer air and lets his tongue hang loosely in a pink frill. My belly button tugs at a thought, as if it's trying to escape, the way it does when you have an abrupt realization that something's happened. Something so atrocious, it can never be reversed. There is a doomed feeling and it sweeps through me with a caustic effect, making me want to puke. My David's not only gone, but he's left me a huge mess to figure out. Where the fuck do I start?

The drive is long and peaceful, enough to halt thoughts of terror. The wind rustling my hair and the sun resting on my arm is subtle, normal. I feel sad that I feel normal. I know that grief is a journey, a long and difficult journey that snakes between normality and depression, smiles and tears, guilt and finding reasons to not feel guilt. Today's chapter is of anger, danger, and confusion that needs to be ironed out, softened, and rationalized, because if I tackle it like this; an insane person, I'll bury myself in fear and immobilize myself into a corner.

The hills look daunting, daubed in reds and browns

and drizzled with pale yellowy-green. Small rocky crags gash their silhouetted smoothness. Everyone's at work save for a lone hiker, already a good way on his ascent, just a black figure against the earthy tones, slowly climbing. I like the feeling of being alone, at one with nature, at its mercy. The scent of summer passing through the mountains and the sound of nothing but the breeze on which it's carried is so very restful.

On my journey up, I pass several crags, stone sheep folds, a wind farm, and lots of rough terrain. I have a sinking feeling in general, a hopeless void that’s threatening to take me under if I don’t find a balance, a way to restore my logical thinking and gutsy attitude. It’s always been a gift of mine, confidence. The only time I felt that I didn’t have any was when I worried about David, about losing him. But that debilitating fear is alive now and playing out like an old scratched record.

I think of him dead, burning and alone, and I can’t quite believe it. I never see his face in those thoughts and my instinct, even though everything points to his death, doesn’t believe it.

My thoughts walk me up to the summit. My head’s heavier, foggier, instead of feeling lighter. The time seems to have sped up, so darkness is already descending. I have to make my way down in the dimness. The fading light plays tricks with my eyes and

I think I see a person, off in the distance, coming down a gently declining rock face that will eventually cross my path. He seems to have come from nowhere, a slight figure moving quickly, rushing like a lone ant left behind looking for the trail.

I have no power in my legs. I freeze, heron-still, my breathing chaotic and more rapid the closer he gets. I hold my breath as he marches toward me, not slowing his pace, his faced hidden behind a balaclava. I tense myself ready for an attack to my surprise, he walks right past me, nods, and continues down the track. He shouts back, "It's getting dark. You shouldn't be up here. It's dangerous." Slumping down onto a rock, I take a deep breath, then I take a few minutes to sort my head out because it's seriously hurting, throbbing. I'm so relieved he wasn't a murderer or another attacker. I hurry down, quick, light steps, hopping, zigzagging to avoid rocks and small stones that are becoming invisible. When I reach the car, I just sit in the warmth, happy to be down, happy to be alive, and ready to tackle my nightmare head on.

FOURTEEN ~ Can anyone hear me?

Lucinda's washing the pots, her sleeves rolled up, a stack of dinner plates at her side. I grab a tea towel and start to dry. She hands me soapy plates. I dry them. We do this silently for a while.

"When I was clearing out Margery's the other day, I found some adoption papers in the attic. I think they're David's." A plate slides out from between her fingers and smashes onto the tiles. The noise is terrific, amplified to sound like the sea crashing. She looks at me as if she has seen a ghost. I watch her eyes shifting from the floor to my face.

"Lucy, did you hear me?" She nods but doesn't speak and I see she's thinking frantically behind those big brown eyes; her mind is winding out panic.

"What's wrong? What is it?" I persist.

"Err, nothing. It's just a shock. We would have known. Are you completely sure?"

"Margery adopted a baby boy called Seth. He was six weeks old. He was adopted on the 19th September, David's birthday. According to the documents, the birthplace, time, mother, and father, were unknown."

"So, that wouldn't have been his real birthday? It would have been six-weeks prior to that date. Maybe, they weren't David's papers. Did you ask Karen about it?"

"I didn't think it was the right time. What if she didn't know? Can you imagine, after losing your brother and mother, finding out that she might be adopted too?"

"Now you give a shit about her, after the way she's treated you all these years?" It's there again, irritation, but this time I confront it.

"What is your problem? Why are you being so niggled lately?"

"I'm just as upset as you are, Rosie. You seem to forget, he was my friend too and to think he had cancer and had all these secrets. It's so bloody upsetting." I look at her in disbelief. I've never heard her like this. She begins to sob into her hands and I sit her down, feeling wary of what she might say next.

"I'm sorry, Rose; it's been a tough week at work, with that young lad attempting suicide and with all the mystery and talk of death. I'm sorry. It's just got to me. Ignore me."

"Of course, I'm sorry too, I'm putting on you. Perhaps it's time I went back to the house?" She jumps to her feet and rushes over to me. Her arms reach around my middle and squeeze me tightly. The faint trace of her perfume feels like home. She places her head into the hollow of my neck and breathes me in as she does the kids.

"Don't go, Rose, I'm being a selfish shit. Please stay, Buttercup."

After several wines and some time with the girls in the garden, we seem to let go of the words, but I still feel a little something. I don't want to tell her about the death-threat. I don't think she could handle it. All these years she's been the strong one. It's strange to see her weak and I begin to wonder why. I've relied on her durability for so long it feels wrong for her to be vulnerable. I don't like it. It frightens me.

***

Forgetting to drop a letter at the post box or to pay a bill or to put the milk back in the fridge, are all normal things. To forget seven years of one's life altogether is a total mystery, even to me. What makes you forget the most fundamental part of your life, your formative years?

On my way to meet up with Ewan, on the pretence I want to talk about the future of the business, I intend to stop by Two Quays and get Anna's side of things first, to see if the two stories tally up. I want to find out who Ninny is and why the old man hates me so. I need to see who's tricking me and find out the reason behind

Ewan's and Anna's relationship, and if it has anything to do with David.

My fretting, while Lucy flips bacon in the pan goes unnoticed and I discreetly slip her car keys into my pocket.

"Rosie, don't even think about it. Wherever you need to go, I'll drive."

"Do you have superhuman hearing or something?"

My annoyance turns to amusement as she replies, "No, Buttercup, but I can see your reflection in the splashback tiles."

"Are you going to come clean? You're not talking to me and I can see you're getting into a mess. What aren't you saying, sweet cheeks?"

"I'm off to tackle Ewan about Anna and I want to pop by Two Quays to see if Anna will tell me the truth about her connection to David."

"So, why are you so intent on going alone?"

"Space, Lucy. I need space outside of myself and you to just think."

"I should be offended but I think I know where you're coming from. I don't mean to crowd you. I just worry, that's all."

"I know."

"Promise me, if you start to feel unwell, you'll stop and call me."

"Promise."

"And you'll be careful, not push too hard?"

It's hard not to snap. Harsh words are at the tip of my tongue, itching to tumble and lash out and tell her I'm not a fucking child.

I make polite excuses, get out quick, and drive toward Cardigan. While passing a sign to Saundersfoot, I come off route, suddenly craving a sea view and to be near water. I have an inexplicable urge feel it on my skin. Walking barefoot in the sand is the perfect antidote for toxic thinking and emptying a crowded mind. I think back to the day in the garden where I saw the old man pottering about. He must live with this Ninny, who I presume to be an old woman, perhaps his wife, or even a dog.

The beach view is breath-taking and empty, save for a skinny man marching along the shoreline with his big yellow dog in tow. The morning sun is warm on my face and the sound of the sea lapping gently at my feet is calming. It's exactly the right place to be, still, perfectly still, looking across silvery buoyant water, listening to the transient sounds of quietness. The serenity of the day has an unexpected effect. I realise I'm standing with my feet in an inch of clear water and it takes a moment to sink in that I'm not afraid of it. I'm somehow drawn here today. I usually stay away from the shoreline, having a sense of dread whenever I hear water, especially the rushing, crashing kind. I determine that it's more the sound that scares me, not the water itself and I find that this remarkably strange discovery is such a relief. I bend down and let water pass through my fingers and the soft movement feels like a milestone, as if I've unlocked something. It feels as though a small cog in a larger machine, that's yet to come to life, is slowly moving.

When I pull up to Two Quays, Anna is outside chatting to Tom. They spot me and give me a warning glare, then hurry inside. For a moment, I contemplate running, but know if I do, I will be kicking myself all day. Anna is arguing with Tom about something. His hands go up in the air and he walks into a side office and slams the door, getting the attention of a young couple sitting with an agent. Anna rushes over, puts her arm under my armpit, and marches me over to her desk.

"I see you're intent on causing trouble."

"What trouble is that?"

"Nosing around."

"Am I likely to find something?"

"Not anything that will make you happy." She looks at me and her face softens.

"Why should you care whether or not I'm happy? You don't know me."

"I know enough."

"Yes, it seems a lot of people know my business. My husband was very good at sharing."

"David loved you very much and had your best interest at heart, Miss Love."

"Miss Love?"

"Sorry, I'm getting muddled it was my last client's name." She points to some papers, then shuffles them into a drawer.

"What are you doing with Ewan?"

She gasps before she can think, then her look shifts. You would think I just asked her who she'd murdered.

"That is none of your business. We are good friends, nothing more."

"Lies. I saw you kissing." My voice must be high because all the staff turn to look.

"For God's sake, woman, keep your voice down." Flustered, she tucks her hair behind an ear to reveal a red spot blossoming on her neck.

"Tell me what the fuck is going on here? You have no right to keep back things that concern me"

"Tell me, Rosie, why would my love life concern you? Now, if you don't mind, I have work to do."

She rises from her seat, as if she's about to leave. Before I realise, I'm at her side, gripping her upper arms, squeezing them tight, daring myself to cause bruises to appear, cover her pale skin with marks. It scares me how much I enjoy the thought of inflicting pain.

"No, you fucking don't, not this time." I shove her

into a side office and lock the door behind us.

“Talk!” There is definite fear lurking in the depths of her large blue eyes, the same look that was there the day I first saw her, a strange mercurial contempt.

“He was helping me do business, personal business and it just happened.” She’s shaking and looks unnerved.

I raise my hand to touch my scar and she finches. Her eyes flutter as if she's expecting a slap. I like the confidence her weakness gives me.

“How long has it been going on?”

“About a year.”

“Did David know?”

“No, he wouldn't have liked it.”

“Why?”

“Because he was protective of me.”

“Do you know how crazy that sounds to me, his wife. Why would he be protective of you? What are you to him?” I slam my hand on the wall and pain rips through my arm.

“Look, you're getting yourself into danger. Please believe me, Rosie I don't want to see you come to any harm.”

“Who would harm me? The old man, your father? Why on earth would he have a grudge against me? what aren't you telling me?”

“He's not just any old man. He’s not someone to

mess with. I honestly don't know why. Only he and David know the reason, but he has warned me to stay away and not ask questions. My father is not someone to ignore."

"My god, you're scared of him too."

"Who else is scared of him?"

"Tom."

"When did you speak to Tom? Stay away from him, do you hear me? I've tried to be nice, but you are messing with fire. Go back to your nice little life before you get burned." Now, she pushes me against the wall and brings her face so her nose is almost touching mine. I admire her for it.

"Stay the fuck away from my family. He will kill you if you don't." This time there is something wild in her eyes. I fumble with the door lock and leg it to the car under no illusion she would do anything to protect her family, including killing me if she needed to.

No better off, I continue the long drive to Cardigan. Ewan is showing a young suave type around the Yard. He's wearing a linen suit and eyeing the yachts with interest and cleaning his shades with his t-shirt. Ewan sees me, gives a little wave, and points to the office this time, they're expecting me and there are biscuits laid out next to the espresso machine. A fraudulent smile is about Wendy, who again, looks nervous.

"It's good to see you," Wendy says, while faffing

about with a file that is obviously intended for our meeting.

"How's Lucinda and the kids? Are they all holding up?"

"Yes, we're all just living day to day. Who's the guy with Ewan?" I'm eager to talk about something else. The concern is bad enough, but when it's fake, it's unbearable.

"Not sure. He turned up this morning asking about David. He said they had been in contact about the yacht that came in last month, *The Mariner.*"

"Did Ewan know about it?"

"He didn't seem to, no."

"That's odd."

"That's not all that's odd. I'll let Ewan explain properly, but we found some documents."

"Documents?"

"David was planning to sell up. He never told us." My eyes drop to the floor and focus on the lines in the wood and how uniformed they are, while my brain catches up and instinct tells me to stay calm.

"You didn't know either." She's not fooled by my calm exterior and I shake my head.

"But he was telling me how well the business was doing, said the yard was flourishing."

I can't fathom why he would want to sell. It was his world, his own little empire. The company had given us a good life. My thoughts turn to his meeting in Scotland. Could this have been the reason? Was there a potential buyer from up that way?

“Two Quays was handling the sale, their commercial side. The paperwork was all drawn up ready for our signatures.”

“I don't know what to say. What did Ewan have to say about it?” I keep my shock to myself.

Anna again. What is this mysterious woman up to? I'm so flabbergasted. I make my excuses and go to take sanctuary in the toilet. I thump onto a loo seat, and sit for a while, trying to comprehend this news. When I get up, I bang my forehead gently, repeatedly, against the mirror. The impact is directly on my scar. I enjoy the dull pain. My right sleeve has slipped back, revealing faint scar-lines on my wrist from rebellious teenage years.

I remember how the pain used to make me feel, as though I had control over my life. The release was euphoric, but suddenly followed by shame, the bittersweet conundrum of figuring out one’s tumultuous life.

FIFTEEN ~ Visions

"You should get that seen to." Lucinda looks at the bruises on my hands and winces.

"It's nothing. Do you fancy a ride out to Pembrey? Mowgli needs to stretch his legs. He's getting pudgy. Aren't you boy?" I fluff his ears and he plonks his head in my lap. I look up to where Lucy's standing, and something strange happens. The wall behind her, the blue wall David painted, disappears and is replaced by a dirty stone wall. It's a brief flash of moss on stone, but hellishly frightening. The room alters for only a second, but fear grips me from my insides and my stomach flips. Lucy looks at me funny and turns to where I'm looking but doesn't remark on my lost look.

"Yes, why not? we could both do with some fresh air." Her smile is big, and I detect relief at my offer of 'us time'. I'm relieved too because her voice brings the room back to normal. I make my way to the bathroom and splash my face with cold water. I can't help but keep an eye out for signs of otherworldly stuff. When I return to the kitchen, she quickly grabs her phone and car keys and we set off, both eager to be out of the house. Mowgli pokes his nose out of the open window as we spin along the hedge-lined country lanes, his tongue lolling out.

"Looks like he's enjoying it."

"He's always loved the wind on his face, a proper happy camper." He sneezes, shakes his face, and saliva splats across the rear side window.

"I don't think I've seen a dog sneeze before."

Our laughter is such a surprising sound, a rich genuine guffaw. I'd forgot how much we used to laugh. I know lately, the world for both of us isn't normal and I'm betting it never will be again.

"So, what did you get out of Anna?" She asks tentatively, as she does when asking the kids why they didn't do their homework. The question, although perfectly normal, irritates me. I find myself feeling uptight, impatient and I'm not sure if I should let my anger spill out and speak my mind, or keep my insidious side hidden. I'm good at keeping secrets even though I'm not sure quite what they are, so I stay cool.

"She threatened me. Said if didn't stop nosing, I would get hurt." I try to keep my voice rational.

"That's just crazy. It sounds akin to something out of a bloody mafia movie."

"Do you think we should go to the police?"

"No, instinct tells me that would only cause more

trouble."

"But what if you really are in danger?" She taps her finger on the steering wheel. The sound of it is loud, annoying and I push her fingers away from the wheel, causing the car to swerve.

"Rosie, what are you doing?"

"The noise, Lucy, I can't stand it."

"You're having a breakdown, Rose. You need help. Why don't we go get you to the doctor later, get some Valium or something to steady your nerves, eh?"

"Don't be patronizing, Lucy, please. My husband's dead. I'm discovering stuff about him I didn't know, every fucking day, something new. I think I'm allowed to feel a bit edgy!"

"Okay, I'm sorry. It's hard for me too. You're my friend. It's a struggle to see you suffering and you're so damned independent. It's hard to watch, Rose, and not want to fix you. I've fixed you before, but I sense resistance, as if you don't need me anymore." She pulls a sad face, her lips curling downward.

"I'm not bloody-well broken. I'm trying to work out an entire life that might have been completely false. I'm not having a meltdown. I'm trying to figure out the biggest puzzle I've ever come across and there are so many missing pieces. I'm at the centre of it, somehow. So, please, allow me my space. I'm not being distant, just doing my best to take the information in. I'm gathering and processing it without crumbling. You must get that, surely?"

"So, let me help." Her eyes are soft, exploring. I can't explain to her that I suspect she's somewhere in this puzzle too. I just have a weirds feeling that she's that small interconnecting part. The one that's usually missing when you complete the puzzle. The frustrating little bit that you'll never find. There's something in her glances, remarks, and impatience that I've never seen before.

"Okay, I don't want to pressure you. Just know I'm here, if you need to run through stuff." It's a relief for the sea to come into view, a wide expanse of deep blue, flat and sparkling. The widest yellow beach is sprawled out, just waiting to get lost on.

It's big enough to walk and walk and not bump into another soul, no matter how many dog walkers are about. The wind whips gently around our ears as we stroll along, coats flapping. The roar of the surf makes it difficult to talk, so we just put one foot in front of the other and breathe it all in, the seaweed, salt, and distant barbeque smells.

Mowgli runs and spins and is generally playful, nose down, bum in the air, sniffing anything in his path. The time out is calming, and Lucy slips her hand into mine, a reassuring little hand. Our silence is comfortable and takes us three miles in a loop and back to the car.

Standing on top of the sand dunes, I spot our car and notice broken glass is sparkling on the ground all around the driver's side. The window has been smashed and something in my stomach pulls on cords of fear, making me feel weak.

"No, no, no." Lucy shouts and runs and tumbles down like we used to as kids. We race to the car to find our phones gone, and a small envelope on the driver's seat with my name on it in writing I know but can't place.

My legs won't work, and dizziness makes my mind spiral out of control. The slipping away feeling descends and my lips won't open. A paralyzing numbness makes me mute. I grab onto Lucy as I slide to the ground, taking her with me. The whistling comes, so loud, so echoey, I cower from it. The shadow lurking in my memory steps out of the dark and the face is blocked by the sun. Why can't I see his face?

***

I'm told later, when I wake at the hospital, that I screamed so loud people rushed over to see what was happening before I had another huge seizure. The doctors ordered total bed rest for a gruelling and boring week and then, as part of my recovery, suggested swimming, a relaxing and not-too-strenuous exercise that would help to rebuild my strength, and with today's warm weather it's the perfect day to escape there to where tranquillity has become my ally.

The pool has an aqua hue that wiggles and shimmers across the walls. It's relatively empty. I come here when it's quiet and not full of kids doing messy swims with splashes and noise. I've become so intolerant of noise.

Slipping in, I dip under to customize myself to the coolness; the chlorine-tinged air has become a welcome smell. Goggles help me find the clarity I get only when under water. They bring a special kind of undiluted focus to a secret world where you can look at everything and no one can see where your eyes are aimed. I love the distance I feel from the world when under the water, a muted and calm place where stranger's legs kick out behind them in an array of styles. I feel weightless and powerful at the same time. I have been coming regularly and it's been a Godsend. My mind has restored a little of the confidence I was beginning to lose.

After my usual fifty lengths, I stay at the deep end for a rest and grip the side while adjusting my goggle straps. I let my head fall back into the water and feel myself sink down, like a brick so my feet anchor at the bottom, like I used to do as a kid. The water's so clear. At the other end of the pool are a group of legs belonging to old ladies however, one pair are small, young and are coming out of a white costume, with big pink roses all over it. They're kicking and thrashing at the water. Maybe, she's a grandchild of one of them?

I shoot to the top to see the girl, but there are three women and no girl. I duck under again and look. There are four pairs of legs, but out of the water, just the three women stand chatting. I'm so sure, I swim over to them and ask, "Where did the girl go that was with you just now?" They turn to one another as if I'm barking mad.

"Dear, there is no one with us." One woman with cotton white hair looks sympathetic.

"You must be mistaken; it's just us, the wrinklies." One of them teeters behind her hand. I know she was there and feel as though the world is conspiring to trick me. I get to Lucy's just in time for tea and tell her about the girl. She suggests I go have a lie down and I lose it in front of the girls, which I've never done before.

"Stop telling me what to fucking do. I don't need to lie down. I'm not insane and I'm not seeing things. She was there, a real girl in a swimming costume with pink roses on it. She was there, Lucy." She disappears into her bedroom and comes out holding a costume belonging to Sky, white with large pink roses all over. It's hooked over her finger and she looks sad. I can't articulate anything because I suddenly feel sick.

"What's happening to me?" I collapse onto the soft bedding and curl myself into a ball.

"Stress, Rosie, that's all the doctors said that you

would go through lapses of memory and might have visions because of the medication. Just take it easy, my lovely. I'm here, always here. OK? Now, rest and I'll finish making tea. I'll shout you when it's done." I lay listening to the bustle of pots and pans and the kids arguing about a dress. I think about earlier and maybe she's right. My mind is having a field day with me, playing all kinds of tricks. I should take it easy. So, I let myself go, sinking deeper and deeper into a sleep that is so solid and silent and restful, it's hard to wake up. When I do, its two days later.

Miss Love, the name rolls around my mind and I say it over and over. The more I hear myself saying it, the more familiar it sounds. I don't believe Anna made a mistake at all. I think she was trying to tell me something. Another cryptic clue.

I've made my mind up that today's the day I approach the old man. To hell with the danger. If Lucinda knew my plans, I think she would probably try to lock me in my room.

On my journey up the hill to *Sea view,* I get stuck behind a tractor and find myself having an impatient hot flush as it chugs up the incline, spitting out straw and raining muck onto my car bonnet. The driver is wearing a flat cap and a pale blue and white checked shirt. He's peering in the mirror, looking at me, his stare unwavering. Without warning, the tractor stops and it's as if all the birds on the trees fall silent and the clouds stop moving. He jumps out and I know before he turns. It's him, the old man. I'm completely stuck. A van behind me starts beeping because he's blocked the road off. He walks toward me, his face fierce, lips pursed. He picks up a branch and lifts it as he approaches the car, intent on doing damage. The man in the van jumps out and shouts, "Oi, what the hell are you doing?" The old man brings the branch down, scattering leaves and debris, making a large dent in Lucinda's car.

"Get away from me. I've warned you, bitch." His voice is high and breaks with fury and veins are ropey on his thick neck. The man manages to prize the branch from his grip and talks him back into the tractor, but he looks behind him, a final glance. My heart is hammering in my chest; like it's trying to escape. To want to attack me in front of a stranger like that, with no care, must mean he's incensed just by my presence. Why?

"Are you alright?" The man says, trembling slightly as he brushes leaves from the car.

"Do you want me to call someone?"

"No, it's fine. I'll be okay. We have history. It's nothing to worry about."

"Didn't look that way to me."

"Really, I'm fine."

He drives away, and I pull into a lay by further up

the hill. I reach into the glove box to see if Lucy has left any cigarettes. The brown envelope is there. I can't believe I forgot about it, or that Lucy didn't open it while I was in hospital. It seems impossible that she wouldn't be curious.

The envelope feels light, so I assume there is not much content. I'm surprised to find a scented, pale-yellow piece of paper with very familiar, spidery writing on. It says:

'Isabelle Knot. Find her and you will have the answers you need. She is the key to unlocking your past. Be careful, your life is in danger.'

There is no signature and nothing else, but, for some reason, it feels like I've won the lottery. An actual name. I don't even care who wrote the note. I presume friend, not foe and my instinct says it's Anna. I roll the smooth paper around my fingers, letting my mind linger on the name; Isabelle. I say it over and over. I feel like I should know it.

I also think about the letters I haven't read in the box from the attic. At first glance, I had presumed them to be other official documents relating to the adoption, but maybe I missed something. I decide to go to the boatyard to have another look around the office. I know Ewan is out with clients this week, so I'll be able to snoop in his office.

For reasons I'm not sure of, I keep this information from Lucy. There's a nagging doubt coiling itself around my inner mind, telling me I need to be guarded, even from her, my best friend. I need to be clever and find answers soon. So, I can call off this suspicious voice and be free of demons.

I park several streets away and proceed to the boatyard. It's empty. Everything is locked and the tall mesh gate at the front is closed. I only have the office door key, so I have to climb over the fence and make a dash across the concrete courtyard to let myself in.

Walking toward the office, the cool corridor is eerie and deathly quiet. Every step seems to make the narrow space grow longer. I begin to hurry. Running from the past, from memories of me and this place, but they catch up with me. I think of David as if he's been illuminated by the sun. I see him clearly, handsome in his pale-blue suit, exuding importance and smelling musky, expensive. It's the day we are due to meet our first prestigious client and he is teasing me.

"Rosie Morgan, are you wearing underwear today?"

"You have got to be kidding. What here, now? They'll be here in a minute."

"Did I ever tell you how sexy you look in that dress?" He approaches me from behind and kisses my neck, softly, butterfly light. A tingle spreads across my skin. He has a way of making me fall under his spell. There's something about his touch, the way it sends a vibration through my entire body, a sensation I've never known before him. He calls it his magic touch and we joke about how cheesy that sounds but it's true.

I'm holding a bunch of files, clutching them to my chest. He slips his hand under them, turns me to face him, and they scatter across the grey carpet like ripped pages from a book. We don't care because we are so caught up in the moment.

His eyes are difficult to avoid, their blue intensity; they hold me there, looking at him, as he expertly unclasps my bra and runs his lips across my shoulder. He lifts me onto him so softly, so gently, with such strong hands. It's there, against the wall, we climax, minutes before we greet our very first clients at the door, looking dishevelled and wearing mischievous smiles.

I have stopped running now. The grey carpet is rough against my legs and my face is wet. I have been strong, avoided the memories, blocking them out because of the terrific pain they will bring, but today I'm caught in the misery of remembering. The grief makes me howl because there is no magic touch anymore, or warm tender kisses, moments of sheer passionate bliss. Here is just an empty, cold, corridor with an itchy grey carpet and me slumped against the wall. I feel as hollow as a cave. I hear a car door. I wipe my tears and run to the window where Ewan is getting out of his car with Anna. The sight of them is so unexpected that I spin around looking for somewhere to hide and find the only place to be the stationary cupboard under the stairs.

The sounds from inside are muffled, but not enough to hide their heavy-breathing, fiery lust.

“We have the place all to ourselves. Board room?” There's a pause for kissing. Their bodies thump against the wall and small crumbs of plaster rain on my hair. The thought of sitting through sounds of animalistic passion in this dreary, cramped space brings on the beginnings of panic. The darkness threatens to overcome me, so I dig deep, think of summer and sunshine and clear morning air. I keep my eyes firmly closed as the lovers perform a dance of sexual pleasure right next to my head. I'm thankful for the abrupt quiet as they groan to a halt and shuffle about rearranging themselves. They make their way to the side office.The chairs scrape, indicating they are sitting at the table.

“That was something, eh?” Ewan’s voice is satisfied, deep.

“Yes. Do you think we should stop?”

“And why would we do that?”

“Because, it's wrong, selfish. Your wife doesn’t deserve it.”

“My wife isn't in love with me.”

“Neither am I.” Anna’s laughter fills the small room. “I've never understood the need for love. Why is sex such a bad thing to want? It's not a crime. It’s necessary. Ewan, you know this is a casual thing we have, benefiting both of us. Why go spoiling it with talk about love? Are you going soft on me?”

“Because, I have feelings for you.”

“No, you don't. You are simply filling a void. The feelings we have are not the kind to base a relationship on. You love your wife.”

“I'm not sure I do anymore.”

“Trust me, you do. Now that's enough soft talk.”

“Did you find out what happened to the letter for Rosie? It's strange it would have disappeared from my house like that.” Ewan’s voice carries a trace of hurt as he muddles through the conversation.

“You sure you've not misplaced it, left it somewhere?”

“I’ve guarded that letter for two years. Why would anyone want her to know about Isabelle, now?”

“Whoever authored it intended her to find out and whoever stole it from me must be the same person.”

“But, why? It’s not going to do her any good knowing. David went to great lengths to keep her from the truth. It's lucky he found the letter before Rosie did. Can you imagine what it would do to her mind? David trusted me with that letter and I have no idea who took it? I should have burnt the bloody thing."

"Could it have been Tom?"

"No, what reason would he have to take it? Come to think of it, Rosie did say he pushed her over on the beach, but I presumed it was because my Dad had given his thuggish, Nazi orders."

"That bastard needs sorting. The sooner we get on with the plan, the better. He should have disappeared a long time ago, evil cunt."

"We'll get on with the plans next week at the meeting with the Poles."

"Does Tom know anything?"

"No, it would finish him. He loves his grandad - if only he knew."

"Let's hope he never finds out." Anna's voice thins to a whisper.

"If anyone knew what that man's been capable of over the years, they would help bury him alive."

"Ewan, we have to be careful. Now David's not here to oversee things, we must keep arrangements exactly as they were, no changing anything. It has to look like an accident."

"It will. We'll sort out the final details with the Poles. They're good at this stuff, the best."

"Can I see you again, this week?"

"No, it's best we don't. We don't want to arouse

unnecessary suspicion. Let's meet as we discussed, at the docks, 8pm, next Tuesday. I want to get this drama over with so Tom and I can take over the business, have a new start, and be free of the old bastard once and for all."

"When you get your share from the sale of the boatyard and your wedge from me for your excellent services, you can retire; maybe, even patch things up with the wife."

The quietness suggests they're gathering themselves, processing words from their damning conversation. I keep my hand tight across my lips, suppressing a definite squeal.

Did I really just listen in to a murder plot? As the door clicks, their footsteps crunch toward the car, and the security beeps finish, I burst out of the confined space, desperate for the toilet, but too lifeless, too paralyzed to move. I lay on the fusty carpet, taking big breaths and trying to stop the words as they spin, around and around above me on a surreal merry-go-round.

Disappear. Evil cunt. Nazi. David was involved. What had this man done to make his family turn against him and who the fuck is Isabelle?

I let my eyes rest above, focusing on an unusual red and black moth that's landed near the ceiling light. Once my breathing has returned to normal, I saunter to the car, exhausted. A sudden lethargy makes my legs feel like concrete. I realise my dress is soaked in my own piss and the smell reminds me of being a child, but I don't know why.

I debate whether to share this information with Lucy and decide that this time, I will. Because at the minute, I'm doubting my own sanity and need to make sure I'm not going crazy. Lucinda is at least good at that, making me feel safe.

SIXTEEN ~ The Past

It feels peculiar, unwelcoming, being back at our marital home. Early morning shadows cast blue lines across the carpet making the house feel cold and gloomy the building has a kind of bleakness to it. It's lost the optimistic lustre and therefore, its appeal. I know I'll have to move on soon.

The thought of using Two Quays to sell my house amuses me. My laughter cuts through the silence. It sounds unfamiliar. It's been way too long since I let it escape and the joy of it makes me feel instantly guilty. I cry, but my ever-present anger insists I wipe away the tear. There's too much unresolved business to waste time on self-pity.

Sitting at our table for two, our carefully chosen bistro set that catches the afternoon sun, I think of us, sipping on our espressos and eating fork fulls of lemon polenta cake, talking idle, familiar talk, laughter caught in the air. Those thoughts are immortalized in my memory. They tug at my stomach and I feel sick, alone and empty. That anxious feeling gnaws at my insides like an army of rats, feasting on my insecurity.

The noisy clatter, as I place the box on the table, sends birds scattering from the trees. I run my fingers across the carvings of maple leaves and into the grooves of mango groves and wonder about the artisan who had crafted such a curious box.

I take out the aging yellow letters. The gold ring is heavy in my hand and shines garishly under the early morning sun. It's big, like an American sorority ring or the kind a traveller would wear. There's a faint whiff of cigars on the paper, a pleasing smell, that puts me in mind of Christmas and foster parent number three, Maureen Alsop. A woman who liked a thin cigar after the twice-experienced boxing day buffet. Her husband had terrifying, impulsive rages and moaned about every morsel of life. Especially the noise of the telephone ringing.

“Oh, for God's sake. What now?” He would bellow and thump his ham fist on the table, making everything jump, especially Maureen.

Maureen was a timid and kind woman who went out of her way to spoil me, love me, and buy me the world. Something my well-practiced attitude hadn't prepared me for. So, I rebelled and fought her every act of kindness with a wall of hatred. I had an ingrained disbelief that I deserved only bad things, and that somehow, if I relented and let myself be cared for, kindness would be swiftly taken away. Girls like me, orphans, didn't deserve happiness.

The letters are all folded into three sections and are so old the creases are wearing thin, which leads me to believe they were read often. The first is a letter from a woman claiming to be David's real mother. I can't help feeling that the mysterious content is another clue to the reason behind his death.

Margery,
You have my son.
You have my precious boy and I'm so very glad he has fallen into your safe, loving hands, just as I wished. It is sad to think I won't see him growing, but that good fortune is impossible and for reasons I can't explain. You see, he was created from an obscure kind of love that wouldn't be understood.
Please tell him I love him and didn't give him up easily. The decision to give him a better home, give him a better life, was determined the day he was conceived. As you know, the adoption papers, the ones that you found in his basket with him, are fake. I'm responsible for this. You were chosen carefully. I know that you took my son with the certainty that it was illegal to do so. But I'm glad, so glad that he is with you, having a normal life and, that he is given love and a chance at normality, whatever that might be.

This way, I'm able to watch him from time to time, from a safe distance and admire him at every stage in his life. I cannot thank you enough for that. For not handing him in to the authorities and keeping him close to me.
I followed you for a long time while I was pregnant. I watched you play with your daughter and loved how gentle you were with her. I saw you walk the woodland path every Tuesday and planned to leave my newborn there for you to find.
I watched from beneath the foliage of trees on that sunny morning, as you carried my boy away to safety, you were wearing a yellow dress. I cried tears of sadness and absolute relief.
My boy will be five now. I hope you are not alarmed by my sudden letter. I have no intention of ever making contact with him. I simply couldn't. I just wanted you to know how grateful I am for your unending kindness.

Yours sincerely

The other letters are much the same, all from her. One is from when David would have been sixteen, and two more up until he would have been twenty, there are no more after. They are revealing and whoever she is, she's not far away. Her eyes are still watching her son grow from the periphery of his life. I wonder what the obscure love is she speaks of that wouldn't be understood and my mind goes to sinister scenarios.

The click of the garden gate startles me and I'm surprised to see Karen. By the look on her face, she's taken aback too.

"What are you doing here?"

"I'm checking the place over. I thought you were at Lucinda's. I sometimes come over, helps me feel closer to David and I'm keeping your plants alive." She looks to the floor. Her whole being has an aura of exhaustion and sadness around it, making me sympathetic toward her.

"Karen, I know we've never seen eye to eye, but I'm really sorry for what you're going through." She looks puzzled by my sudden compassion.

"You don't need to say anything. We've both had our share of shit to deal with recently. Let's not pretend we're ever going to be best buddies, okay?"

"Agreed."

"I want to ask you something. It might be difficult to hear, but there are too many secrets surrounding David's death and I need some clarity."

"Go on." Her face becomes curious with the lift of a thin eyebrow.

"Did you know David was adopted?" Her expression is one of scepticism and her laughter creases her forehead.

"Don't be absurd."

I push the adoption paper and the pile of letters over to her. I watch as her eyes volley down the pages, eating up the words in absolute disbelief and horror.

She doesn't make a sound. Tears flood her eyes and the papers fall from her fingers, as if she has no strength to hold onto them.

"I'm sorry. I was shocked too. Did your mum ever say anything at all?" Karen shakes her head, gently, gawping at me through streams of tears.

"I don't understand. She used to talk to us about our dad all the time, said he was a hero, loved us to the moon and back. She never let on, ever. Do you think I'm adopted too?"

"Maybe it was to protect him and no, you were already three when he was adopted."

"But he had a right to know. You don't think mum's death had something to do with this?" Her eyes grow wide with alarm.

"No, I don't. I think she was grieving and in a very bad place."

I can't tell her about the threat because she is too fragile and I'm certain she would mess things up and steam in, causing chaos with a barrage of tears and unthought-out rages.

"It doesn't change anything. He's my brother and nothing can alter my memory of him." Her face says otherwise, a slight tightening of the lips and a pinched look about her.

“I'm trying to piece together what happened leading up to David’s death. Is there anything you can think of, anything he said that was unusual?”

“There is something I thought of the other day. David was so placid. I saw him at the boatyard arguing with a young man with blonde hair, a big man with broad shoulders. He was shouting and saying that he didn't care about something. The young lad spat at David's feet and David punched him on the nose. When I asked what it was all that about, he said, ‘It’s nothing, it’s just a customer that’s refusing to cough up’.”

It has to be Tom, the young man. What on earth was going on with that lot? What mess was he involved with? I pretend to be as clueless as Karen.

“That sounds odd, but he did get the odd ranting customer.”

The deflection goes well. She gets up to leave but turns back, sharply as if she’s about to say something.

“Are you OK?” Her sincerity brings a smile to my face.

“Yes, I'm doing OK, considering.” She nods her acknowledgment and quietly clicks the latch on the gate.

SEVENTEEN ~ Isabelle

Isabelle is the next piece of mystery to unravel. I like the sense of purpose I feel knowing I have a plan, a slice of hope to hold onto, even if I'm doing it alone. I think of ways to tell Lucinda I'm going to be away for a while, so I can go up to Scotland and try and re-trace David's steps and find this woman, who I'm sure will give me a solution to my quest for answers. She doesn't take the news well, fretting, worrying, as if I'm another one of her kids.

"You can't go away now. You're too vulnerable. At least let me come with you." Her eyes plead with me but I'm all out of reasoning.

"No, I need to be alone and just get away from it all. A short break will do me good and I can take care of myself."

"Tell that to your doctor. You're supposed to be resting, for God's sake, Rosie!"

"Don't talk to me like I'm one of the kids, Lucy. You've no right to be so fucking patronizing." I see hurt flicker in her eyes before they turn red.

"I have every fucking right. You are under my roof and I am responsible for you. Do you understand how important it is for you to get well? I care. Forgive me for fucking caring. You've hardly been yourself lately."

"Well sometimes, friend, I wish you didn't care so much!" My voice is loud, sharp. The kids come in from the lounge to see what's up.

"Mom, why is Rosie crying?" Sky asks.

"She's having a down day. We all have them sometimes. Now, go watch TV." Her voice is quiet. I leave without looking at her.

David's car is losing his smell, and my stomach lurches. I try to picture his face on the morning he took me to Cardigan to see the offices. He was dangling the four-leafed clover charm in my face as we sat in the driveway.

"Today is a special day, Rosie. This is going to bring us all the luck in the world." His eyes were so sincere. I let the chain fall through my fingers, then wrapped it around the rear-view mirror. It's been there ever since. I tug at it now, suddenly angry and the chain snaps. I keep pulling, snapping and snapping until there is nothing but a pile of silver chain pieces in my hands. I toss it out of the window.

"A lot of fucking good that did, hey David!"

My flight to Edinburgh is delayed. I have time at Cardiff Airport to drink coffee and Google Isabelle on my phone. It's not long before her face pops up for her Facebook page. She's young and pretty, possibly oriental with long glossy, black hair and angled dark eyes. The first thing that comes to mind is a daughter, another secret. She's too young to be anything else. I doubt she is a business colleague. She looks more like a student. I laugh at my Miss Marple approach to my trip and let my brain settle on my bustling surroundings. People's muffled conversations are all around me. I need for my mind to remain calm, so I mute the fervour and noise. I'm going to be alone in a strange place. I need to keep my thoughts logical and do a methodical step-by-step plan of my stay. I have to find her. I can't go back until I do. My phone buzzes in my pocket and Lucinda's message makes me smile.

"You stubborn donkey. God only knows why all the secrecy, but I'm sure you have your reasons. Be safe and stay in touch, please."

When my flights called, I get up and notice a man with a big frame, square-shouldered and very little neck. He looks over at me and smirks in a menacing way. He could be Mexican, mafia, he's so intimidating. He strides toward me in a long black coat and I take a step backward as he reaches down to my side and picks up my suitcase.

"It looks heavy. Let me help you." His smile is so puppy-dog wide that I laugh at my ridiculous paranoia and thank him. He smells very familiar. He's wearing the same aftershave as David. He rushes off with my case and I struggle to keep up with his gargantuan steps.

"Wait, please, slow down." How does he know which gate I'm going to? He stops just shy of my gate, places my case down and turns to walk off. He isn't smiling anymore as he glances back at me, his eyes cold and mean, penetrating.

"Enjoy your trip, Rosie." he shouts back in a broad Scottish accent and my brain freezes. I seriously doubt my mind could handle any more questions about mysterious people, so, on the flight, I bury the big Scottish brute to the back of my mind and tackle the journey ahead.

By the time I've landed I have an address and a taxi booked to take to Linlithgow, a town a few miles out of Edinburgh. There's no time to waste. I need to find her. Although something tells me she'll be expecting me, just as Anna was. My steps are monitored from somewhere and my concern by whom, is becoming a worry.

The taxi ride is long and beautiful. We speed through some seriously drastic countryside, Autumnal colours bursting across the hills and rock formations silhouetted against fading sunlight. It's how I imagined Scotland to be, colourful and dramatic. I picture

Isabelle with my husband, on these lanes that wind past a loch and palace. I wonder what their conversations were about. What brought my husband here? Was this girl involved in the murder plot? It seems incomprehensible. Could she have been part of a chain of people that were somehow connected to the old man. The Nazi cunt?

We pull up to a row of set-back cottages, smoke billowing from wonky chimneys. My B&B is shabby, paint peeling from the door and ivy creeping over one side. There is no sign, no way of telling if they accept paying guests. There is just a plaque saying, *Woodlands* on a wooden gate which squeaks at the hinge as I push it to get through. The curtains in a large bay window are moth-eaten. No one answers the door. I walk around to the kitchen and see an old woman busying herself with a pile of carrots and a peeler. I watch her for a while before tapping on the window.

She waves me to the door, looking at me cheerily as if she's seen an old friend. It takes no time at all for her to tell me she was widowed three years before and that her husband died suddenly, in the room I'm to be sleeping in. I'm not sure if she's kidding or not. I sense a wickedness about her.

That night, in the room I lay out my findings so far. There are so many pieces of paper and photographs that they take over the floor and bed space. It's impossible to connect it all up.

Isabelle's piece of paper is in the middle. Red ink marks her out as the most important piece of all of this. David's car accident was three miles from here and tomorrow, I will stand on the spot he took his last breath, before I go to confront Isabelle. Go to face the truth.

***

The coordinates on my phone tell me that I'm at *the* spot. I'm at sharp turn in the road. There are faint tyre marks veering off from the road and onto a grassy verge. There are still indentations where the tyres made deep grooves, but grass is growing, and time is covering the tracks.

I feel nothing. My mind won't let me go to that day. It seems impossible that something so tragic could have happened right here, something so devastating that it could cause a crater of emptiness in my life. It's so tranquil, beautiful even. After the S-bend the road is straight, a line of grey, flanked by marshland and rusting ferns, as far as the eye can see. A bird of prey circles above and comes to a halt, hovering and watching, focusing intently on something on the ground. I shield my eyes, just as the bird swoops down, talons out front and wings begins, it's magnificent, and close enough to see splayed bronzed wings and a flecked breast. It tears at something with its beak and I see a flash of red and rodent fur and a brief squeal before the silence.

Not far from the site, I spot a dark patch among the ferns. As if it's been scorched. I struggle to walk on the ground, trying to avoid turning my ankle on lumps of mossy earth and small gullies. It's boggy ground and I imagine it would be hard to start a fire here. It's further than it looks and by the time I reach it, the road is a way back. It looks like a recently used campfire, large stones placed in a circle. A responsible fire builder was at work here, but why? It's so remote and not a tourist area. Among the surrounding ferns there's a small piece of material that is torn, as if it's from a shirt. It is blue and white plaid. It looks out of place against the autumn palette of grasses.

I reach for it, but I stumble over an unseen mound of peat and land on my backside. Wet instantly seeps through my jeans and there's mud down my right leg. I tug at the material to free it from the fern. I run the embroidered emblem of a rose between my fingers and my mind wakes up. It's David's.

I tell myself to breathe. I can hear my heartbeat above everything else. I struggle to see straight, so I slump against the cold wet earth. there's a trickle of water coming from an underground gulley and I watch as a bird flies off, eastward. The sound of water is so loud, amplified as if it's being piped through a speaker.

It's so bad and I can't make it stop before he comes. There's a shadow against a door frame and a hat, on big shoulders. Behind him is a dim light as he whistles the same tune, always sombre. I can't move my hands to cover my ears because I'm paralyzed. Warm comes between my legs as I wet myself, the stench permeating my nostrils, terror keeping me still. The shadow lurches forward, as if he's about to take a step. Then, I see a car, skidding, screeching, and spinning, around and around. There's a dark-haired woman in the passenger seat, her face pinned to the window, terror in her eyes, screaming, but I can't hear her.

David is slumped over the steering wheel, being thrown left to right, his head thumping the window. As the car skids to a halt, both of them are propelled through the windscreen with such force they land on the grass limbs, splayed awkwardly like broken dolls. The woman's eyes are wide open there is, a trickle of blood at the corner of her mouth. David's face is caved in at the nose and mouth. He's lying on his side, facing the woman, neck broken. There's no doubt they are both dead.

I tell myself again to breathe. I count my way back to consciousness, as the sky once more turns cloudless blue and I find movement in my arms and when I sit, the world turns the right way up and I know.

He wasn't alone. He was with a woman. It has to be

Isabelle.

This wasn't like other flashbacks. This was different, as if I was watching a movie, but I know it was real. The ever-present shadow, that deafening, macabre melody. What are their meanings? There has to be meaning to the haunting sound that's becoming more and more frequent. I'm so afraid of it and the terror that lurks behind it.

I hitch a lift back to the B&B and manage to get to my room before the dotty landlady spots me looking ghastly, dirty and covered in my own piss.

After a shower, I lay silent. The tap drips and I muffle the sound with a towel. I get onto the police and ask the sergeant that came to my house if David was alone. He confirmed that he was, but I know that's a lie. Everything is becoming a fucking lie. I scream into a towel so that the crazy woman can't hear me.

***

After a trail of door knocking, trying to trace Isabelle, my search stops at an ornate canal boat on the Union Canal. It's well cared for, flowers and plants spilling over most of the roof and hand-painted watering cans hanging along the side. The boat's name, *Polgara,* is scrawled in gold script along the side, just noticeable under cascading pink flowers. Autumn leaves have scattered along the towpath and there's smoke billowing from the boat. The smell of frying bacon makes my stomach growl. I realise I haven't eaten since I arrived, having slept through breakfast despite knocks at the door. As I'm contemplating what I should say, a jack russell in a red neckerchief jumps at the window, startling me. It barks, and Isabelle looks through the window and smiles and waves. She carries on cooking, obviously used to people walking by and having a nose. I continue to watch her move about her small kitchen. All kinds of scenarios play out in my head, David slipping his arms around her waist while she cooks, like he used to do to me. I find a tear has made its way to my chin. She places her plate on the table and notices I'm still there, standing motionless, frozen. She walks across to the door opening and pokes her head out. Her hair is tied back with a scarf. She's older than she appears in her photographs, maybe mid-thirties, which makes the possibility of her and David being lovers a possibility.

"Can I help you?" She asks.

"Are you Isabelle?" I reply. I don't see any point in wasting time with pleasantries.

Her expression changes from curious to suspicious. I know the look well.

"Depends, who's asking?" she answers, trying to do a mock laugh, but I have her covered. Her eyes are speaking to me.

Her smile disappears when I ask, "What was your

connection to my husband, David Morgan?" The pulse quickens in her chest. Between the collars of her checked shirt, a small visible throb gives her away. She seems to have the same look Anna had when I first met her, like she's fearful of me. She waves her hands, gesturing that I should leave.

"I'm sorry. I don't know any David Morgan. You must be mistaken." She swiftly closes the door and subsequently all the curtains along the length of the barge. I find a nearby bench to sit on next to an old fella wearing a grey, flat cap. His hands are gnarled with time and his eyes are reduced to no more than pale blue holes pushed deep into a doughy, crepe-paper face. His smile through watery, flack lips, seems genuine.

"Beautiful day for a stroll," he says almost to himself. He peers up at the cloudless sky, then brings his eyes down to the trees lining the tow path as they shiver off leaves that sway to the ground.

"Yes, it's a lovely day," I reply, glad for the friendly voice. He leaves shortly after, waving behind him, his frame too stooped and arthritic to allow him to turn. I find myself thinking how I got into yet another bizarre situation. I take my notepad and pen. I scribble my number down with a suggestion that we meet, as I've no intention of leaving until we do. I decide to give her a day to mull it over before calling in on her again. I leave the note tucked in a plant pot outside the door.

I make my way into a small town, a fifteen-minute walk from the canal, and find an antiquated tea shop that looks down the length of a cobbled street. I lodge myself in a window seat where I refuel on piping hot tea and scones to give myself time to recap on recent events. Shortly after I've settled at my table, a man enters. He looks familiar. After a few minutes, I'm convinced it's the same gargantuan man from the airport.

He orders a coffee and makes his way to the back of the tearoom, around a bend where I can't see him. Curiosity gets the better of me and I sum up the courage to go and confront him.

"Er hem, excuse me, aren't you the guy who carried my suitcase at the airport?" He looks over his *Sunday Times* and then around to see if I'm speaking to him.

"I'm sorry, dear, you must be mistaken. I, err, haven't been to the airport." He lets out a hearty laugh and something inside of me snaps. How dare he mock me?

"Don't play fucking games with me? I know it was you. I'm sick and tired of all this mystery. Who the fuck are you?"

I remember the man at the airport had a small tattoo on his wrist, a swallow in flight, and I suddenly realize that this isn't the man. It's too late. A security guard from a shop across the street is escorting me outside, just as the man's wife turns up wearing expensive perfume and wondering what's happened in the five minutes she left him to go buy a magazine.

I try to explain to the guard, but he tells me to leave, like I'm some crazy person. I walk through the streets trying to make sense of everything and just as I turn into the lane to the B&B, my phone buzzes with a message from Isabelle.

"Meet me at the cottage by the old train tracks, 5 pm. Izzy."

After quizzing several locals as to where this might be, I find myself, some forty minutes later, dropped off in taxi, down a farm lane, outside of a derelict cottage that is so tangled in nettles it's hard to see the where it begins. Isabelle's waiting outside, looking apprehensive, a scarf coiled tightly about her neck. The wind makes her hair take flight behind her like she's underwater. For a second, I see Lucinda's face, but I put it down to weariness.

"Why such an isolated spot?"

"It has meaning, here. It used to be my Mother's. It was she who contacted David."

"What business did she have with him?" I follow her eyes as she searches her mind for words.

"She had letters belonging to someone David knew."

"What letters?" My knees are weak and my body trembling. *She better not fucking lie to me.*

"I don't know what was in them. She never spoke to me about them."

"Great, more fucking mystery. Come on, you must know."

"This was her cottage. She left it to me when she died and whatever secret was in those letters was buried with them both. I know they met many times, and spent a long time talking about whatever it was, but honestly, I have no idea what they were about." Her eyes are telling the truth, but it still leaves me with questions.

"So, you know about David's death?" Her eyes drop to the floor and my curiosity reignites."Please tell me you weren't fucking him?"

"I wasn't, I swear, but we were friends. He had business up here and after meeting him at my mother's we became friendly. We would meet up for coffee from time to time. I swear that was all. He spoke about you and Lucinda all the time."

"Lucinda?"

"Yes, your sister."

"Lucinda's not my sister, she's my best friend."

"I must have gotten mixed up. Listen, I really don't know any more than that. David was a lovely man, but I can't help with anything else. I'm sorry."

"Do you know where the letters are now?"

"My mum gave them to David, just before she died. My mother was a very secretive person. She kept them right up until the last minute. It was the day after her funeral that David had the accident."

"So, they would have burned with him?" She detects the desperation in my voice.

"I'm so sorry you had to come all this way, truly."

"Is there anyone else who might know what the letters were about?"

"I did hear them, once, talking about Carton Hayes, an asylum my mum worked at before she retired. Something about a resident she worked with, but I've no idea if that's connected."

I scribble down the name of the asylum and thank her for meeting me. The taxi is blinking yellow lights into the fading day.

"One more thing. Did you know David had cancer?"

"Yes." It's almost a whisper and the realisation that she knew cuts like a knife. *Was I the only one he didn't talk to?*

Isabelle jumps into her car, squinting at the rear-view mirror as she speeds off. I go back to the B&B and drink more wine to help me sleep before my flight in the morning.

EIGHTEEN - Canal Boats and Questions

Something has altered in Lucinda's demeanour, a shift in the way she carries herself. She would usually turn to greet me with big smiles and bags full of welcome curiosity about my trip as soon as she heard the door. But she continues to stand at the sink, rubbing away at rust-coloured stains from a roasting dish. She lets her gaze flicker to the window and rests her eyes on the skyline.

"Hi honey, I'm home," I say, hoping to bring a little warmth into the room.

"How was your trip?" she inquires with about as much enthusiasm as a sloth.

"Everything okay?" I ask, sensing tension.

"Yes, everything's just fucking dandy!" She says, still not turning toward me. She dries her hands on a tea towel and throws it onto the worktop. She turns then and walks toward me, swiftly, as if she's gathering momentum to come over and strike me. I cower as she gets close.

"Obviously, something's wrong, Lucy. Tell me

what's up," I say.

Her face unchanging, she snarls, "Why did you go up to Scotland without me?" She's close enough for me to get a whiff of sour alcohol on her breath and I notice the empty bottle of Merlot on the table.

"Where are the girls?"

"My Mum's. Why the fuck, Rosie? Don't you trust me? Are you hiding shit from me? Do you know how irresponsible you're being and bloody selfish? I'm here going through my computer and find flight ticket receipts. Do you know how worried I've been?" Her words are drunken, slurred.

I know I deleted everything, left no trace of my trip. How could she possibly have found out? She's too inebriated to challenge, so I decide grilling her is best left until the morning. She flops into my arms like a rag doll as I usher her upstairs to her room.

"Wanker, you are, a bloody wanker." She thumps onto the bed and stares at me with glazed eyes.

"You're being ridiculous, Lucy. Get to sleep, we'll talk tomorrow."

"You need to get a grip, Rosie Morgan, seriously. I saw a post comment from Isabelle: 'Safe trip.' Why would you stir up that shit, why? It's dangerous. Don't you see that?"

She cocks her head to one side and penetrates me with a cold stare. It takes me by surprise.

"You fucking amaze me, Rosie," she says.

"I need you, Lucy. Don't you turn against me too, not now," I say whispering.

"You always need me. Do you have any idea how bloody draining that is?" She's tearful. She's also piqued my interest and I try to ask her more, but she's out of it, snoring, obviously too drunk for serious talk.

I return to the kitchen. It looks like she's been robbed. It's a mess, stuff all over the worktops. Lucinda's usually a neat freak, so I presume her pity party had the better of her.

How did she know about Isabelle? Unless, she opened the letter and sealed it again, but that wouldn't make sense. She said 'dangerous'. What could that mean? She knows something. I'm certain. I rattle my brains to try and find a link between Anna, Ewan, and Isabelle but come up with nothing. In the lounge there's more evidence of a drunken night. an ashtray with squashed dog ends and a tipped wine bottle that has bled red wine onto the rug. The log burner is smouldering and a couple of embers flash before dying off. Under the sofa, I think I see the corner of the remote and I reach under to slide it toward me. It's the phone, the bat phone. Why would she have it? There are photos on the sofa, one singled out from the pile. It's the three of us at school, me, her, and David. His arms are draped over her shoulders and she's staring up at him in complete adoration. I'm staring directly at the camera. I don't recall this photo. I've never seen it before. I turn it in my fingers so that the back is facing. The writing stops my heart:

'Lucy 4 David 4ever' with a heart drawn around it.

She's kissed the photo with her coral lipstick. I must be careful not to read anything into this. There are a hundred pics of us all together. We were close. Maybe, it was just a joke? Maybe, it was innocent fun. It has to be. It's an impossible scenario, them together. I would have known. I run up the stairs and stand in the doorway of her bedroom, watching her snore lightly with the picture in my hand. I get close to her face and slip my hand under her pillow and slide it from under her head. My head is pulsing with excitement. I lift it and imagine it over her mouth, cool white cotton over her nose, her legs kicking out, then stillness. I allow it to drop close, so her warm breath is dancing on my fingers. She rouses.

"Rosie, what the fuck?" Lifting her head, I place the pillow under her.

"You were snoring. I wanted to lift your head." I leave quietly, frightened by how good the thought was, how natural to feel so normal and yet, aroused around such wicked thoughts. I find my fingertips tracing my scar.

"Lucy, how did you know about Isabelle?" I whisper

as I leave. "I never told you about her."

"I looked her up after seeing the comment she posted about it being a weird day, getting a visit from a stranger. I saw she was from Scotland." I know it's a lie because that doesn't equate to being dangerous, nor does it explain her rage.

I wake on the sofa with a crooked neck. Aching as if I've been run over by a truck. My dreams were surreal, about the letters and a stark white room, about what new secret they might have contained.

Lucinda appears in the doorway wearing an apologetic smile. Last night's clothes. Her hair is dishevelled, her lips wine stained.

"Thanks for cleaning up," she says, scanning the area.

"My pleasure. What was all that about last night? You were hostile, Lucy. I'm not used to you being like this?"

"I was pissed. It was probably a load of nonsense. I apologise for whatever I said, OK?" She looks suddenly sad.

"What is it?" I ask.

"A case I was working on, that young lad. He took his life yesterday. I guess I didn't cope well."

"How?"

"Hung himself at the unit."

"Lucy, I'm so sorry. I had no idea."

"Why would you?" she says, quietly.

I have the question churning around in my head. I want to know about the photo and I can't quite get my head around the fact that she got all the information about my trip to Scotland from a couple of remarks on Facebook. I also know that my recent collection of paranoid thoughts could be contributing to my speculation.

I make us a bacon sarnie and a pot of coffee. I squeeze her hand and say nothing. When our cups are empty, I ask, "How old was he?"

"Sixteen. Still had his life ahead of him. It's just so sad." Her eyes fill with tears and I pour us another cup. We remain silent some more. There are only certain people you can be silent with, no need for words, because the feeling of empathy is enough.

I head off down the beach with Mowgli and soak up the smells that I associate with home, the bittersweet sea smells and the distant scent of the farm fields. I'm a way along the golden half-mile crescent of shoreline, my collar pulled up around my cheeks to stave off the chill. My mind is still in Scotland. My phone vibrates in my pocket. There's a new message from Isabelle:

"I forgot to say, David mentioned a Mrs. Love once, when he was chatting to Mum about the asylum. When I came into the room, they stopped talking, but the name stayed with me. Not sure if that's any help? Izzy X."

I run the name through my mind and connect it to the time Anna had called me Miss Love by mistake. It can't be a coincidence. David must have told her something.

Jellyfish have washed up along the shoreline. They are mostly upturned circles of translucent rubber, with alien-looking faces set deep into them, like they're trapped under glass. Maybe aliens have been here all along?

On my way back to the house, it occurs to me that I haven't spoken to her about the murder plot. Maybe, I should let her in on everything, perhaps she can help me after all. It won't be long before she trips herself up.

When I arrive, Lucy's pulling her coat off the peg.

"Where you off to?"

"I've gotta pick the girls up from my mams and I desperately need headache tablets," She smiles at me weakly and is out of the door before I can speak.

I shout after her, "Have you heard of a place called Carton Hayes, an asylum?"

She doesn't need to answer. What little colour is left in her cheeks drains right out and her eyes spring open, just enough to give her away.

"What is it? You look shocked."

"It's nothing, just feeling a little peaky. Yes, David mentioned it once to Karen in the garden, those two were always talking. He said he had been around that way once and that it was a creepy old place. I'm not sure why I remember that."

"That's it? he never mentioned going there?"

"Not that I recall." Her smile fades. She gets into the car, I'm guessing, to avoid more questions and my gut instinct tells me she's in on whatever is going on. I decide to pay a visit to my deceitful sister-in-law.

Karen is in her garden, pruning. She's lost a significant amount of weight. Her skirt is resting on her hips, revealing a knuckle of hip bone, as she reaches up to snip at branches that are already sheared to nothing.

Lately, I find myself holding back, watching people, as if I might glean something, a secret. Perhaps a behaviour that's only carried out in private. I find myself wanting to catch someone out at something. Maybe, so I can prove that I know when foul play and deceit are about me, just as I know the dark envelops the night and keeps the world dormant. She notices me as she turns to pick up a rubbish sac and stumbles backwards into a naked, thorny bush.

"Bloody hell, Rosie, you shouldn't sneak up like that. You gave me a fright." She's flushed, her cheeks seeping red. She takes the corner of her cool-blue linen shirt and wipes her brow, leaving mud smears.

"What brings you here?"

"David. Scotland. Have you ever heard him mention the name Isabelle?"

"No, please don't tell me there is more strange news. I don't think I could cope."

“Not bad exactly, just a bit of mystery.”

“What kind of mystery?”

“David was visiting Isabelle’s mother up in Scotland. She had letters, concerning me. I don't know what was in them. Do you?”

The question catches her off-guard and she blinks quickly, something she does when nervous.

“No idea. So, that's why he was going to Scotland. How did you find out?”

“A letter was left in the car, on the car seat. Someone smashed the window when me and Lucy were at the beach a few weeks ago.”

“That's bizarre. Who would have known? Why not just hand you the letter, or talk to you?”

“I've asked myself that question time and time again. Your brother had a lot of secrets.”

“Do you have any idea what they would have been about? It must have been important for him to travel all the way up there.”

“I don't have a clue. Apparently, the girl's mother worked in an asylum. Isabelle overheard her mother talking to David and I know that he mentioned it to you.”

“Yes, I remember something, but it’s foggy. He said a lot of stuff. Have you been to check it out? Did you get the mother's name?"

"You know, I didn't. How extraordinary, I didn't think to ask."

"Maybe you should."

"Whoever she was, she's dead now. That's why David was there. It was the day after her funeral that he had the accident."

"So, he must have known her well then, to go to her funeral."

"I really don't know, but I have to find out. Will you help me?"

"Isn't Lucinda helping you? I thought you two did everything together."

"She has her own problems at the minute."

"It's not like the golden girl to have problems."

"What's that supposed to mean?"

"I thought she was perfect, immune to problems." The comment is loaded with sarcasm and it throws me off what I'm saying. I've never noticed a rift between the two.

"I thought you liked Lucy."

"What's not to like, right?"

"Whatever, she's a good person," I say.

"You think so?" Her reply is icy.

"Do you know something I don't?"

"Just that she's a jumped-up tramp."

"Rubbish, she's one of the most genuine, down-to-earth people you could meet."

I feel anger surging from my stomach to my head. Before I know it, I'm tearing at her shirt. She jumps out of my way and crashes into the newly painted garden fence.

"What's got into you? Are you bloody insane!"

I claw at her face, enjoying my impromptu rage, and feel her skin concertina under my nails. The scraping sounds satisfying as I scratch at her pale skin. Pink lines surface on her cheek, pin-pricked with blood.

She pushes me away and runs into the kitchen. Locking the door behind her, she turns to look at me through the glass, ashen, shaking. I enjoy how I feel, powerful, in control. Her weakness is my drug.

My euphoria begins to blur with visions of a wall, the same stone wall I always see, covered in swathes of moss. Water appears through the cracks, like a thousand tears of glass and the whistling begins.

The garden swirls up to the sky, twisting into a frightening darkness that descends, and forces me down onto Karen's lawn. There's blackness. The sound of water is close. It's suddenly cold and I see an arm, splayed out on the grass, a child's arm, dirty and bloodied.

Terror speeds through my veins and I can't escape. I'm pinned to the ground. There's no air for me to take in. I'm sinking, sinking, sinking, into the grass. It's closing over me and then, nothing.

I feel a tapping, tap, tap, tap, on my face. Light creeps into my dark place and Lucinda is staring down at me. *A dream, just another dream. Karen's OK.*

"Wake up sleepy head. We'll be late for our date with Anna."

It takes time to focus, time to adjust from dream to now. After a second of being totally paralysed, I smile up at her. She's sliding back the curtains, a halo of sun behind her, her smile warm.

"You were making some pretty strange noises in your sleep. You must have had one hell of a dream."

The coffee mug Lucy hands me is hot on my fingers. I try to remember the fading nightmare, but it's escaped, as most of my dreams do. Once I fully come around, I remember I had spoken to Anna with Lucy in the background, egging me on to push her for answers. After I told Lucinda everything about my journey, so far, and my thoughts on the situation, she suggested we crack on and push for some long overdue answers, together. She also suggested that I trust her wholeheartedly and stop being a paranoid idiot.

There's a warm bath waiting for me. I slip in and wash my skin roughly, wash my hair vigorously, and splash my face with water. I sink under to rinse off the suds. My head slides along the bottom of the bath, its dark, really murky, mud is swirling around and I'm unable to lift my head. I panic, desperate to breathe, but I'm pinned down again. The whistling sound is loud, louder, louder. I see a hand coming for my neck. The menacing shadow of the whistler is above the water, ripples hiding his face, behind him is a sunlit sky. Terror forces me to open my mouth and water floods in. Lucy yanks me up and screams, "What the fuck, are you tryin to kill yourself?" I cough out water and sob while she slumps into a corner,

"Lucy, I'm scared. That wasn't me. I couldn't move, it was as if someone was holding me down."

She shakes her head, "It's all connected to David's death, post-traumatic stress disorder. It does funny things to your brain. It can even bring on hallucinations."

To hear the words is like warm chocolate melting away my fears. Maybe, that's it. This is all down to David dying in such a terrifying way. This is all normal. Maybe, it's David I'm seeing and hearing, I feel an instant pang of comfort. Lucy does it again, rescues me. Maybe, I should trust her after all.

NINETEEN ~ Revelations

Anna is sitting at her desk, looking elegant and efficient, next to a pile of unopened folders. Just like the last time. She looks up over her glasses in a way that suggests she's not happy about me being here.

"Not here, let's go out to the pub to talk," she says, getting up and putting her rain mack on. She marches outside, nose in the air and shouts back to her secretary.

"I'll be out for a while," The woman's nails make a racket as she taps at the keyboard. She tosses us a quick uninterested glance.

I follow her, stilettos scratching at the pavement, all the way to The Bryngwyn. I text Lucy who's waiting in the car, just in case I need back up.

"We're off to the pub!"

We find a corner by a roaring fire, a place for a romantic couple, and we both smile at the location.

"So, what do you think you heard?"

"You and Ewan, planning to kill your father, the cunt."

Her eyes close to slits and she picks up her wine and

takes a sip.

"My, my, quite the little spy, aren't we? Did you get a kick out of listening to me and Ewan fucking?"

"No. I was in a panic. When I heard you come in, I hid in the cupboard."

"But, why? It's your company. You have every right to be there."

I have no answer because she's right, so I shrug and say, "It is what it is."

"What you heard and what you think you heard are two different things. First, I'm planning to take my father's businesses because I damned well deserve them. I've been running them all of these years while he's been doing nothing but taking the money and living in that pit of his, in squalor, like a porper."

"So, what was all the talk about the Poles?"

"They are helping us launder money and to set him up. Not that I have to explain anything, but when you accuse me of a murder plot…"

"But he'll go to prison. Does he really deserve that?"

"Oh yes, he deserves to die like a pig for what he's done." There is a genuine flicker of sadness that vanishes in an instant as she fans away a flush with a brochure.

"What did he do to make you hate him so?"

"If only you knew."

"I'd like to."

"I don't know why you feel the need to pry all the time. Look, I'm sorry about David, truly I am, but you need to leave things alone. He's gone."

"He might be gone but he's left one hell of a mess behind. I need some answers, so I can move on. My life's turned upside down and if I can clarify some of it, I can get on with my life."

"Okay, if you really want to know about my father, here it is. When my mother died, I was a little girl of just nine, innocent and heartbroken. My dear mum. His weak and loyal wife took care of everything. He never lifted a finger or cooked a meal. My father was a wicked crook that mixed in a dark world. He was also stuck in the middle ages. He expected his woman to do everything, take care of all his needs. All of them. That responsibility was passed on to me the day she died." Her words take a minute to find their place in my head and when they do, the realisation is harrowing.

"You mean…"

"Yes, until he got too old and ill to bother. I've been planning my revenge ever since, for years. He's an evil bastard."

"So, Tom is his son?"

"Yes." All of a sudden, I see her for what she really is, a broken little girl, and my heart hurts for her. Tears fall openly, and she smiles at me for the first time. Her protectiveness toward Tom now makes sense.

"Ewan knows, then?"

"Yes. It's the first time I've said that out loud to anyone but him. Tom has no idea He thinks he's his grandfather. Now that you know, will you please leave me alone, I beg you?"

"Yes, sure. One more question before I go. Why does your father hate me so much?"

"That, you'll have to ask him. I don't know, honestly." She wipes the tears away and stands tall, sliding her hands down her skirt. She cinches in her raincoat at the waist.

"I trust we're done?" She says, with no trace of the conversation we've just had. I suppose she's hid it all these years.

I relay the conversation to Lucy, who's is in the car warming her hands on the heater as it blows out warm air.

"Fuck, that's some heavy shit, dirty, evil scum. He deserves whatever he gets. My God, what's wrong with some people?" she says, then suggests we get a coffee at the beach and talk some more. Her face is twisted with anger. I feel a strange grey cloud hovering around. Such a bleak story for such a dark, wintry day. My insides shiver at the thought of what happened to Anna, a thought I'm unable to shake for the following weeks.

***

One morning, after a period of rest and forgetting

about things, I remember the bat phone and ask Lucy over breakfast.

"I forgot to ask why you had the bat phone that night you got pissed."

"I didn't."

"But I found it under the sofa, in the lounge. I took it back though."

"I honestly don't remember taking it."

The suspicion in my voice must be obvious because she asks, "You don't believe me?" But I think I do. *Could I have had it in the lounge before?*

It's taking time to build a picture in my mind of how this gargantuan puzzle fits together. I'm slowly letting myself believe that the universe is not colluding to deceive me. There has to be a rational explanation for everything, Isabelle and the letters, Lucy's peculiar mood changes, David and his other life, Karen's keeping of secrets, Anna's maudlin, atrocious life.

It must have been torture living with the knowledge that the son you love so much is the product of incest. The indecency and hatred must be eroding her from the inside. At least she found Ewan, albeit for sex. Perhaps her incest scars run too deep for a loving commitment to be possible. Perhaps she's died inside, a thousand times over. Maybe, she doesn't feel at all.

It all must be part of a world, an ordinary world where abnormal, surreal shit happens, and the sky falls down around you for a short time, but you pick yourself up and deal with it, push the sky back to lofty heights when things calm.

I'm feeling braver, stronger. Is there a momentary lapse in my lifelong insecurity? Whatever it might be, my confidence knows no bounds for the time being. While I feel in control, I have to progress this world of mine to a place where I find peace. Only by finding answers and interconnecting everything, will that happen. I need to approach the old man, show him I'm fearless, look him in the eye, and solve the riddle of his hatred for me. What reason could there possibly be for his unrelenting anger? Guilt, for abusing his only daughter, for looking his inbred son in the eye everyday with both love and disgust? It's a bitter pill to swallow.

Where do I fit into that obscure equation? I've pondered. Maybe, the mysterious childhood that eludes me so, could be a link, but I can find no logical path leading to his door. There's only one way to find out.

I decide to leave Lucy out of this but will tell her on my return. She's still reeling from the death of that young boy, not coping, tearful, and pensive. I'll find the miserable old man that seems so sour faced and bitter. I'll just ask him why, why my face should bring rage and rattle him to the point of wanting to do me physical harm. Could this man be my Whistler? Could he be the key to a door I'm not sure I want to open? Instinct tells me no. It tells me there are more interweaving veins in this complex body of lies for me to travel along before my answers come.

***

The drive to the campsite is slowed by agricultural mayhem and darkened by high hedgerows that block out the brightness of the day. Long shadows precede the car around sharp corners and there's a distinct smell of cow manure scenting the air as I twist and turn through the lanes. I cast my mind back to the day I drove around similar back roads, following Tom. There was also a little light then, and my head had been sluggish, catching pulses of light from the side window, escaping through small holes in the hedgerows. They became rapid the faster I went, like thin lasers directly at eye level. I think that's what caused my blackout, the little blinding flashes. A dull ache begins in my shoulder where the impact of the crash fractured bone.

I reach up for my sunglasses, hooked over the visor, and hope it will abate the flashing spindles of light that hit the windscreen, creating a luminous web of gold that looks like spun sugar, obscuring my vision.

The campsite is impossibly empty. Tall pine trees behind the main reception are scattering a few remaining leaves and a chilling whisper sings through sparse branches. Maintenance men in matching fleeces are knocking in new fence posts with lump hammers and painting surrounding fencing with pungent creosote.

I park on the main car park, sick of hiding away. Brazen in my approach, I walk with confidence toward his ramshackle of a house. This time, I'm not sneaking around the back, but up to the front door, where bulging bin liners are stuffed with rubbish and old clothes. They're piled high next to the door, like he's had a recent clear out. The appearance of the house is shabby and tired. An unloved shack. I'm surprised it's been allowed to get in such a state on such a well-kept sight. It's as if a scorch mark in spring grass, ugly.

I rap until my knuckles hurt. The door swings open on crumbling hinges and a small, dishevelled man stands in a stained vest. His skin, mahogany, leathery, is darkened by many seasons of sun, a pipe cleaner of a man with fierce blue-green eyes.

Before I can open my mouth, a blow connects with my chin and knocks me to the ground. It's too fast to initially feel pain and shocks me into momentary paralysis. He grabs my wrists tightly and drags me into the house, snagging my skirt on an uncovered carpet gripper, before anyone sees. His strength is enormous. He pulls me toward the sofa and dumps me onto it with minimal effort, puffing out dust clouds.

"What the fuck are you doing here, you nosy bitch? I thought I told you to stay away." I'm so startled by this old man's instant violence. For a second, I find my response firmly rooted inside my head, but I'm unable to form the words I need to protest. He takes a moment to scan me, pushing his face close, sour tea on his breath, muck lining deep creases around his eyes. His fingernails aren't much cleaner. He waves a finger close enough to my nose for me to smell old smoke on yellowing hands.

"Cat got your tongue?"

"What is your problem, old man?" I manage.

"You are my problem, you and that crook of a husband you had."

"I don't understand. What did we ever do to you? I don't know you."

"Yes, little miss goody-two-shoes, you know me alright."

My chin is throbbing, my wrists snake-burn sore. I stare at the wrathful face, trying to remember, but there's nothing I recognise.

"I don't understand. What on earth are you talking about? I don't know you. You need to let me go. People know I'm here."

"Nobody knows, Miss Love. You are too secretive to tell people where you are, what you do, isn't that right?" *Riddles, why is he talking in riddles?*

"You are not making sense!" My voice rises because I don't like the control he seems to have. He's dangerous. I can sense the fraudulent calm, quiet of his voice, measured, sarcastic. My mouth is dry, and I know that if I'm to get out of here, I need to be subservient, a willing and compliant woman. Instinct tells me that if I irritate him, it will only aggravate his temper, ignite his predetermined cruelty. I'm wary as he moves around the back of the sofa. I feel him behind me, rancid breath warm on my neck, and quickly get up and move myself over to the kitchen table, where I can keep an eye on him. He pulls out a chair, scraping noisily across the bare floor, and sits opposite me. His eyes are cold, staring at me, unblinking and filled with unrelenting animosity.

"Tell me, how is it you think I know you and why do you call me Miss Love? You're not the only person lately calling me Miss Love. I'm guessing that's not a coincidence. Were you in business with David?" His laughter rings through the air, a sound that makes me want to clamp my hands to my ears.

"That man couldn't do business. He was a snake, a lying, conning bastard. Owes me money. His debt is now yours. I was giving you time to grieve, but you seem to want to stick your nose in."

"Money for what? What was he involved in?"

"You're asking the wrong question. You mean who was he involved with?"

"OK, who then?"

"Me, that's who. He knew better than to fuck with me. I warned him. Mr. Clever Man threw a live grenade in my lap, expecting me to implode. Nobody messes with Old Man Jenkins and gets away with it. The explosion will always be thrown right back."

His mouth tightens into a line, lips white at the inner edges, spittle at the corners. His eyes have changed colour, chameleon-like, dark, forbidding eyes. I shrink back as he leans in and looks me in the eye with a reptilian glare.

"What are you saying?"

"I'm saying, what goes around comes around."

"Did you kill my husband?"

"Now, why would I want to incriminate myself to his little whore? You know you weren't the only one, the only naive tart?"

"That's bullshit. He loved me."

"Darlin, he loved a lot of people and he knew better than to try and rip me off. That's all I'm saying. Now, why don't you get the fuck off my property. I'll be in touch when I'm ready. You best get saving, Miss Love."

I have more questions. He has no patience and throws me out of the door, forcibly, shoving me from my upper back. I flounder, losing my balance, and snap a heel from my shoe.

The door slams so hard behind me it rattles the

windows and the workmen turn to look. I limp to the car and breathe in the frosty air, glad to be out, eager to be gone. I remove my shoes and hurry into the car, feeling his eyes watching me behind dirty net curtains, a hunter letting his prey escape, only to be hunted again later. I'm still unclear. Did he kill David? Is that what he was saying? Did he somehow have a hand in his so-called accident?

Hot tears make their way to my chin and I let them fall, tasting their salt. My hands tremble rattling the car keys, as I try to find the ignition.

My mission to resolve a myriad mystery was a huge fail. The surge of emotion is overwhelming, and sobs come hard and loud before I manage to start the engine. After fumbling around in my bag, I locate my cigarettes and lighter. Once on the road, I make my way home, window down, cold wintry air blowing back whatever smoke I expel. The smell reminds me of a faraway childhood, the verge of a memory that never manifests, but I don't know why. Who the hell was I?

Back at the house, Lucinda notices my unease and rushes over to me.

"Look at you, you're shaking. What's happened?"

"I went to see Old Man Jenkins. Yes, I know it was a stupid idea. He hit me. He's such an evil man."

"You bloody fool. I can see, you look terrible. You'll need some ice on that. You have to go to the police.

You can't let him get away with this." She forages around in the freezer drawer for frozen pleas and then pushes the bag onto my chin, making me wince.

"Don't be such a baby. What did you say to make him thump you?"

"I didn't get a chance to ask much. He pretty much dominated the conversation. Told me I was David's little whore, and not the only one. Said David owed him money, ripped him off, and now the debt is mine. He wouldn't give details. But something he wasn't saying is what's bothering me most. He called me Miss Love. Three people have used that name now. I'm not getting something here, Lucy. Before I was married, my name was Jones. I have my birth certificate. So, why is everyone calling me Love? There's so much hatred toward me from him. It's scary, Lucy, really bloody scary."

"Maybe, he's just trying to scare you off. He's an old grumpy man with a lot of shame to hide. Perhaps he's just toying with you. Think what he did to his own daughter. That's one messed up individual. You shouldn't have gone up there alone. Just think of what might have happened." She looks at me with kind annoyance; she wants to be angry but can't.

"Good God, Rose." She looks at the red marks on my wrists.

"What the hell did he do to you?"

“Pulled me from the floor by my wrists and dragged me into his filthy house, that's what.”

“You must have been terrified. You have to report this.”

“No, I don't need to. His comeuppance is already in motion. All I have to do is sit back and watch the fireworks.”

“Anna and Ewan’s plan?”

“Correct.”

“We do need to find out why everyone's calling you Miss Love though. It sounds like a porn name.” It's nice to see her laugh, the familiar curve of small creases around her mouth. She tosses a wink my way and flicks the switch on the kettle.

“I think we should pay Karen another visit tomorrow and quiz her some more about David. Perhaps she's holding back. Her and David talked all the time. Maybe she knows what kind of work he was mixed up in. Did the old man say how much David owed?”

“No, only that I should start saving to pay him back. That man is a nasty piece of work.”

“Let's hope Anna and Ewan get a move on. He needs to be out of the way.”

***

Lucy and I are back on track, the friendship back to normal. I realise how much I need her. I rest my head on her shoulder and we are silent and comfortable. She strokes my hair lightly, like she used to when we were kids and I was upset. I'm reminded of how that warming feeling was probably the most secure I've ever felt, even more so than during David's hugs and back tickles way into the night. There's something genuinely pacifying about old friendships and the history to them.

After a while we make our way upstairs to bed and I settle into the soundest dreamless sleep. When I wake in the morning, I have a strange sense of calm. It’s as if I know, everything's going to be OK. I check Lucy’s room. She's not there but her bed is made. I figure she's walking the dog. I check the girl’s rooms and they're fast asleep.

I find Mowgli curled in his basket under the kitchen table, his lead hooked over the peg. I check the garden and she's nowhere to be seen. By nine o’clock, I'm getting seriously concerned and call her mam. She comes and collects the girls and takes them to school. I sit and wait. Time shifts to midday and I feel strange, like my good vibes have been scrubbed away by a scourer and replaced once more, with fear.

TWENTY ~ Echoes

There is an ominous echo to everything I do around the house. It's been four days with no word from Lucy.

After informing the police and explaining to them about previous threats from Old Man Jenkins, and the subsequent death of Margery, the cockerel, there's been silence. It's as if they've glossed over my concerns about the old man's involvement in David's death. Perhaps, his power goes deep into the community, even into the police force. Lucinda's mum has taken the kids to her house. I'll never forget the look she gave me as she ushered them into the car, a backwards glance that was loaded with blame. Lucy's work is calling every day to see if there's news. Turmoil has set in. I'm jumping at shadows and flinching at creaking pipes like a nervous cat. I'm suddenly terrified at the possibility that Lucinda's been taken because of me. After locking all the doors and frequently checking the upstairs windows, in case he comes for me, I settle in the kitchen and wait.

The day is overcast. A steel-brushed sky is reflected

on the sea and, although turbulent, it has a gloomy magnetic feel to it that's almost calming. High winds are flattening tall grasses on the dunes and sand is sweeping through the air in miniature swirls. I have a sudden need to feel the cold air on my skin. It's always been a tonic for my unstable mind. Icy, cold air has always made me feel alive, awake, and is in some way restorative. I decide to risk going outside.

The patio doors are taken by a gust of wind as I battle my way out to try and get onto the beach. They crash into the wall and for a split second, there's a chilling silence. Then, a diagonal crack appears, the full length of the doors. I struggle to hold on, but they escape again, shattering both glass panels.

Glass falls about me in giant shards. Smaller fragments rain onto my head and catch in my hair like diamonds. The sound of the frames hitting the wall sends a thought racing through my mind, the same unnerving thought I had when following Tom's car in the summer. I recognise the tapping as the door smacks repeatedly with tempered rhythm onto the wall. Tap, tap, tap. Drip, drip, drip. The sky fades away as I drop to the ground. The doors continue to smash. The wind's lamented cry gets into my bones and my body is frozen, still; I'm fastened to the floor. The sound is alarmingly loud. I can't move my hands to cover my ears. I can't move a muscle. The light dims and he's here, his shadow lurking behind a doorway. My heart is galloping. There's a pressure in my chest, as if someone's sitting on me, anchoring me down. I'm aware that Lucy won't be here this time to find me. Could this be it? Is he going to reveal himself to me? The thought provokes panic. I choke in air and my throat tightens, swelling my eyes.

I don't fight the nightmare this time. I let the dread wash over me, the cold penetrate me. The whistling sound echoes. The voice is clear, deep, definitely male. The shadow has square shoulders and, a tall hat. The steps are in slow motion, heavy, and they rattle the floor planks as they grow nearer. The light behind his colossal frame is artificial, not sun. I hear myself breathing, shallow quick, panicky breaths. His hand grips the door frame and he begins to come closer still, slow deliberate steps. He's bigger than I imagined. He's beastly and there's such an overpowering smell of tobacco. I'm instantly nauseous.

As he pushes a thick arm forward to touch me, I scurry back into a dark corner where an army of spiders scatter up the walls. I search for a face, but there is nothing, just a blur, a pencil sketch of charcoal grey as if someone's scribbled over where his face should be. Water is cascading down a moss-covered stone wall, glistening like running glass. I'm near running water, but I'm also inside a room filled with right-angled shadows, triangle after triangle of shadows. I begin to focus in on a small tuft of pea green fern sprouting from the wall, a single droplet of water at its tip. My light suddenly fades; it's been snatched away, and the man retreats. Darkness descends as I slip away into the hushed depths of unconsciousness.

Bang, bang, bang. The sound invades my sleep. I open my eyes to a night sky, still, star-littered and softer than silk. The doors are gently banging the wall, Mowgli is curled into me. He's shaking but has not left me alone. My head is heavy, throbbing. Crawling in through the doors, I manage to drag myself into the kitchen and slump against the wall while my body starts to come to life and my minds gets its bearings. I reach up to retrieve a glass of water from the counter, but my hands are trembling so violently that I can't hold it. Once my breathing has slowed, I manage to get myself onto the sofa. Mowgli jumps up and lays next to me. I wrap my arms around him, grateful for his warmth. The doors continue to smack, smack, smack against the brick, although quieter, less frequently. I don't have the strength to move and close them. I let myself drift, curled against him, the rhythm of his heart a welcome drum, marching me off to sleep once more.

***

The local radio station is blurting Lucinda's name on the news slot. It's the most stomach-churning thing I've ever heard.

'Local woman, 39-year-old Lucinda Hayden, hasn't been seen since she disappeared from her home on Sunday morning. It has come as a complete shock to family and friends, who are worried for her well-being, and say they have no idea why she might have left. There are growing concerns for her safety and the search to find her continues.'

It's as if they're talking about someone else, a stranger. They give the impression that she's possibly been abducted. The first thing that comes to mind when you hear something like this is, where will they find the body? The words whir in my mind and the unimaginable pain of thinking her lifeless brings bile to my throat, my best friend, gone with no trace, nothing. A woman who would never leave her children. The only thread I can possibly attach to this is stress, her job, the young man that took his life on her watch. Could the reality of his shocking departure have ruptured something inside her? Did she need to be invisible for a period of time in order to cope? Was she sick of looking after me? I juggle with the ideas like they are disorientating balls of hope. I've not eaten in days. My reflection is pitiful, grey, my cheeks sallow. I need to fuel up with good nutrition and get to the Old Man, to see if I can summon up the courage to confront him. I know he's responsible. I know he's dangerous, but I'm also aware that I'm the only one who can approach him. I call Anna, hoping to find an ally, but find she's out of the country. Tom, however, is working at Two Quays, holding the fort, and agrees to meet me. I tell him I want to talk to him about his mum. I don't feel he would agree to meet me if he knew about my fears that his grandad has abducted my best friend.

***

Burry Port’s antiquated harbour is deathly quiet. I wait at the little coffee shop, watch the seagulls jab at the mudflats, and note the thickening cloud and continual smudges of grey sweeping across a white canvass. It's not long before Tom appears, wrapped up in a long, grey, trench coat, with a University-style, woollen, blue and grey striped scarf, tied in the London knot. He looks very business-like and his shoulders are broad. His smart attire doesn't seem to suit his babyish face. Even though his frame is bulky, he looks like a boy dressed up in his dad's clothes. The sight of him emphasises the enormity of my situation. Here is a man who has no idea his brutish grandad is actually his father but does know that he's a very violent man.

How do I go about breaking the news? I need him on side if I'm to enlist his help in finding my friend. I see no other way; I must convince him of his grandad’s involvement without making him angry. I must tell him the truth.

He approaches my table with a straight face. Unsmiling, he sits and clasps large hands on the table, his face showing the intrigue his voice masks.

"I'm on my lunch break, so I don't have long. What's this so-called important news about my mum?"

"I have a few questions first, if that's OK."

"What's with the interrogation?"

His smile is wide, his teeth small and neat, like squares on math papers. His face softens, his manner suddenly friendlier, when he sees my concern.

"Are you close with your grandad?" His eyes grow thin at my unexpected question.

"Yes, but what's that got to do with my mum?"

"I have some information I think you should know about him." He guffaws.

"Trust me, there's nothing that would shock me about that conniving old bastard. I'm aware he's no saint, but he's my grandad. So, if you've come here to tell me some secret about his thuggish history, it won't shock me, or change my opinion of him."

"This might." He focuses in on my face, intrigue continuing to blister in his eyes.

"Go on then, shock me." He sits back in his chair and raises his arms, either side of his head, mocking me with a sarcastic jeer.

"He's not your grandad." The amusement disappears faster than a rabbit into its warren. He furrows his brow, and sips on his *Americano*, blowing to cool it, pausing to take in my words.

"What are you talking about? Are you bloody nuts, woman? Of course, he's my grandad."

"When your grandma died, your mum was just a little girl. She took on a lot of responsibility for such a wee thing. Your grandad put an awful lot of pressure on her shoulders." His bemusement shows as he nervously laughs off my comment and gently slaps the table in jest.

"How does make him not my grandad? You're talking drivel."

"Just hear me out. The duties she had weren't only household chores."

"Look, she was amazing. She looked after him. She's a strong woman. I know she had a hard time as a kid, but that's just life. I don't get what you're trying to say."

"Your mum had also taken on your grandma's 'wifely' duties." These are dangerous words I spill and I'm unsure of the reaction I'm going to get. I flinch when he picks up his cup and lowers it to the table again.

Cogs begin to click. Watching the penny drop is similar to seeing light fade from the day. As he registers my words his face sags with the weight of my accusation. He takes his coffee cup and, without warning, hurls its contents in my face.

"You sick fucking bitch. I don't know what games you're playing, but you better stay away from me and my family. You're a nutter, my mum was right about you."

He runs out of the shop and stops just short of his car. He bends forward and rests both hands on his knees, drawing in deep breaths. He continues to a viewing bench overlooking the harbour and sits, letting his head fall between his knees.

I see that something is happening. He's scrambling around in his head, remembering past arguments from his childhood that never made sense, words said in an alcohol fuelled temper that were too abrasive and disgusting to be true, unpalatable conversations too twisted to retain and process. He's processing them now.

I walk behind him and place a hand on his shoulder.

"You knew?" I ask.

"I didn't want to believe it, thought it was my imagination. I heard some weird things when I was little but didn't quite understand. And now you've gone and made it all real." Quiet sobs vibrate through his heaving shoulders. I leave my hand there while he unburdens years' worth of pent up confusion and grief, shedding tears of shame. He's so overwhelmed that he crumples into my arms like a child. I move around and kneel in front of him. We stay like this until the tears stop.

“What will you do?”

“I can't go back there, to that house, ever.”

“Come to mine, I have more to tell you. There's a whole world going on that you are not privy to. It's time you learned the truth.”

“How did you know about all this?” he questions.

“Your mum. She's been angry with him all her life. I think she found relief in saying it out loud. She was trapped. Kept quiet because she loves you and she didn’t want you to know.”

“What the fuck does that make me? A bastard? A freak? Oh, my God. OH, my fucking God.”

Overwhelmed with emotion, he slaps his palm to his forehead and tears come again. He looks broken, his face blotchy and contorted as he wipes the wet away with a sleeve.

“This is Jeremy Kyle stuff. Fuck me. Can we go to yours, please?”

We continue along the back roads, watching a golden-pink dusk descend over the seaside houses, lighting their windows gold. Such a pretty, fairy-tale sight for such an ugly scene. We take my car. He's in no fit state to drive.

“Can I ask who Nini is? You had just fed her when I came to the campsite that day in the summer. Is she your dog?”

"Nini is my sister. She has learning disabilities. She's in supported living, only comes home at weekends."

My heart aches for him as I learn of yet another child that must be born from incest. What a quagmire of emotion this is turning into.

"Do you think....?"

The sobs return as the grimness of all this comes crashing down.

"She must be his too. She's older than me. That fucker, he'll pay for this, mark my words."

***

While Tom sleeps off his shock in Lucy's bed, I stare at the sky, a perpetual ever-changing painting. Today, mauve streaks and pink grazes shift over a sheet of darkening navy. The beauty of the sky never ceases to amaze me. It's a constant I can rely on.

I stare at the newly replaced windows turned toward natures greatest view in my turquoise, velvet, Queen Anne chair, that's worn from hours of sitting, reading a plethora of beloved books. I enjoy watching day turn to night. Mowgli at my feet and I wonder how I'm going to tell Tom about the next harrowing chapter. Will it send him over the edge? I need to ensure that he hates his grandad just enough to help me, but not enough to make him crazy. After deliberating, as the pinks dissolve into the inky night, I decide against telling him anything else, until he's stronger. One thing I do need to know is if he has any idea why his grandad hates me so badly.

I wait until the morning, after he's polished off a hearty breakfast, to ask. I fill him in on Lucy's sudden disappearance. He suggests that it is more than likely stress related and says he's sure she'll return soon. Before I can open my mouth he asks, "Is that why my grandad or whatever monster he is, was so mad at you? Because you knew."

The torment is etched deeply in the young man's face and I feel every ounce of his pain.

"I don't know. Your mum didn't know either. It's a mystery, apart from him having dodgy dealings with my late husband. Maybe, you could help me find out?"

"I don't think I can be near him right now. I'm scared of what I might do." He shudders away the thought. After much deliberation, I decide that he's altogether too delicate to know everything. His mum and Ewan's affair would crush him.

I leave him to wallow and head over to see Karen, to ask her about her conversation with David about the asylum. Ewan's car is in the drive and for some reason, I sneak around to the back of the house. It seems odd that he would be visiting, because they weren't at all close. In fact, he disliked her as much as I did.

They are seated in the conservatory drinking tea. It looks like a formal visit. Karen's face is grave, as if she's just received bad news. Her face is blotchy, and she has a tissue in her hands. Ewan looks to the floor while he speaks to her and she breaks into a sob. The situation seems uncomfortable. He doesn't move over to comfort her, but instead gets up to leave. She stays for a while, crying into the tissue. Ewan gets into his car and leaves. Whatever news was just broken was not good. I make my way to the front and ring the doorbell.

It takes a few minutes and when she answers the door, there is no trace of the tears I just witnessed. She is blemish free and cheerful, leaving me baffled at her miraculous recovery.

"What a surprise." She looks around behind me, no doubt, to make sure Ewan has gone.

"Yes, sorry for the sudden visit. I wanted to ask you something about a place in Scotland."

"Carton Hayes, you mean?" She can see I didn't expect the direct reference to it.

"Who was the woman David was going to see? Who was Isabelle's mum and what were the letters about?"

"They were about you, of course, and her name was Ida."

"What on earth could those letters contain that he couldn't tell me about?"

"I don't know, but they had him spooked. He said he needed time to digest them, get his head around what he saw in the asylum, before he could deal with it."

“What exactly did he see?”

“That’s the thing I found weird. He wouldn’t tell me, said that it would compromise our relationship, that it would only stir up trouble if I knew.”

“So, why did he tell you anything then? It doesn't make sense.”

“He said that if he didn’t tell someone, he would go mad. He needed to confide a little, however, not enough to give me the full picture. I’m surprised you know about Isabelle. How did you find out about all of this?”

“Lucy and I were out on the beach and when we returned to the car, someone had smashed the window, leaving an anonymous letter. I looked Isabelle up on the internet and went to find her.”

“That’s very brave, to go up there all alone. You must have had a fright, someone smashing your car window like that.”

“Why brave?” She ignores my question.

“I’m guessing the letter also said he and Isabelle were growing close, very close.”

“No, she said the opposite, that they were purely friends.”

“And what did your instinct tell you? She’s young, pretty, David showed me her picture.” A giddiness forces me to sit up. Her words are delivered in an intentionally cruel fashion. I sit back for a little, contemplating the poison Karen is stirring in her malicious cauldron. It seems she's back to her old self.

"I believed her. I looked her in the eye. She wasn't lying."

"I know my brother. He was telling the truth."

"You knew why he was going to Scotland all this time. Why didn't you say something? You saw how much pain I was in, thinking all sorts. Was it to be nasty, a final waft of your witch's wand?"

"Now, now, Rose, you're being a silly girl. It was to protect you; your husband had just died. Do you really think it would have helped to know he was falling for someone else?"

"You were eager enough to tell me about his cancer."

"That was so I could give you hope. His trips away weren't deceitful."

"Yet, they were." She looks out of the window and stops talking for a minute.

"I know that all of this is deeper than an affair. Whatever was in those letters is important. I need to go to the asylum and find out who this woman was. There was obviously something very disturbing about his visits. Why don't you come with me?"

"I have to admit, I'm intrigued, but do you think it's a good idea?"

"I don't know. Did you know about Ewan and a woman called Anna having an affair?" Watching her face grow ashen is like watching someone die, as if I've just punched her. Air escapes slightly parted lips and she makes an almost inaudible sound. She can't keep her face from crumpling. Her eyes fill with tears before she can stop them. There's something satisfying about hurting her.

"No, I didn't," she says and shows me to the door without saying another word.

"Think about the trip?" I say, before leaving.

So, Ewan has been playing the field, getting his oats wherever he can. It shocks me because he's always seemed so family oriented. He's been a loving husband and a doting father - apart from the recent shenanigans with Anna. It seems the world is full of secrets. It begs the question - is he with Anna for her money? Will he benefit from their little villainous agreement? Her father is a wealthy crook after all. Is Ewan a liar, just like my husband?

When I return home, Tom has left. There's a note on the kitchen table thanking me for letting him stay, but saying that he would take it from here. Him leaving has scuppered my plans to enlist his help to retrieve information from his grandad or dad, as it were. I have five missed calls from Anna. I guess he's confronted his mum about his grandad. It seems I've disturbed a live hornet's nest. I take no pleasure in it. He seems like a decent enough guy. I know, only too well, how having very traumatic news can alter your perception of the world. I fear what lies ahead for him.

***

Ewan agrees to meet me at the beach to talk about the business and what we are going to do with it. I've decided I want no part. He can buy me out. I've little interest in it. It all seems connected to David's deceit. I know I need to wash my hands of everything and move on. Once my answers come, I can make new plans.

He approaches my car from the side and lights a cigarette as I get out to greet him, smoke rising into the air in little plumes.

"I presume Anna's told you that I know about everything?" His eyes are mischievous.

"Yes, I don't see why you didn't come to me. We've been pals for a long time. I could have explained."

"You must think I'm an asshole," he says.

"I don't get it. You have a lovely home, stability, a wife who adores you. Why risk it all for a fumble in the office?"

"It's more than that, Rose, I love her. She's an incredible woman. All those horrendous secrets she's lived with all these years. It doesn't bear thinking about."

"And Karen, are you in love with her too?"

"Ah, you know about that?" He grins and sucks on his cigarette.

"Of course, I know, you stupid man."

"Karen was an accident. She was upset about her mum and David. I called over to ask if she'd seen you. I had some papers for you to sign. We had a few glasses of wine. Anna had just told me she didn't want a future with me, not the way I wanted, and we ended up spending the night together. It should never have happened. You can't tell Anna."

"Has the whole world gone mad, Ewan? I couldn't have imagined how all this change could be so bloody disruptive a few months ago. My life was so perfect or, so I thought." He links his arm through mine and we walk along the eerily empty beach, making footprints in virgin sands.

"It's going to take a long time for you to heal. You know that, right?" I don't answer.

"Any news from Lucy? She's been gone awhile. You must be worried sick. Are the kids OK?"

"To be honest, I think Old Man Jenkins has taken her."

"Why?" He looks uncomfortable. A liar's blush creeps up past his collar before the lie comes.

"Because, he's threatened me before. I think he killed Margery as well. He said if I didn't stay away, I would regret it. One dead woman and another missing. I'm pretty sure he killed David too."

"You should you know, stay away. That man has

serious connections. He's far too dangerous for you to be poking him with a stick." The lack of empathy confuses me. David was Ewan's best friend and he didn't pick up on the fact I just said I knew who murdered him.

"Is it possible he has Lucy?" I ask, looking for the liar's blush, but it doesn't come.

"I don't know, but I can help you find out. You need to stay out of sight. Let me handle this. If he does have her, she's in danger. You have to keep your head down, OK?"

"When is it going to be over, your plan with the Poles? That would solve everyone's problems."

"Not yet. This could have an impact on our little mission. I need him to not be thinking about anything other than our fake business venture. It could spoil things. If he gets a snifter that something's wrong, we're done for. I'll follow him around for the next few days, see if he goes anywhere off the beaten track. I doubt he would have her at the house. Is there any way she could have just taken off, to clear her thoughts? Her and David were close. Maybe the whole situation has messed with her head?"

"It's not likely that she would leave her girls alone like that."

"They weren't alone. They were with you."

"She knows I'm useless with organising the girls.

There's just no way."

There's an unfamiliar noise above our heads, a buzz, similar to the sound of an electricity pylon on a wet day, a penetrating noise that makes us both look up. There's a small drone with its nose pointing directly at us. I scan the area to find its owner, but there's no one standing up on the sand dunes. Save for an old woman and her troop of yappy chihuahuas, the beach is empty.

"That's weird. Nosey sods. They should ban those things," Ewan says, looking cautiously about him and hurrying me forward. We stick two fingers up at the whiny contraption that continues to stay with us for the next five minutes. It seems like a lifetime. Ewan directs us toward the sand dunes, where we can escape the thing in a derelict military bunker, where women used to make weaponry during the war while the men were away. The drone stays, watching, to see if we come out. Ewan lights us both a cigarette and eventually, the noisy contraption goes away.

"Bloody kids got nothing better to do, probably." His laugh signifies he's shaken.

"You OK?" he asks.

"Yeah, of course. It's bloody cold. Shall we head back?" The wind picks up on the way to the car and he pulls me close. The familiar smell of musky aftershave is comforting, in the same way the scent of washing detergent smell makes you smile and think of home.

My car is adjacent to a forest entrance. The trees are lofty and still have a smattering of autumnal leaves at their tops. At the opening is an ochre path that starts wide and thins out, leading deep into the forest. The wind is wild and knocking the trees about. It's beautiful, entrancing.

After Ewan leaves, I stay for a while and take some atmospheric photographs. I notice a way into the shadowlands there is a slim, dark figure. It could possibly a leaning tree branch that looks similar to a man's silhouette. The object is an interesting, dark shape. I position my phone, so the light picks it up. The leaning tree steps out onto the path, startling me, and comes toward me, slowly at first. The figure starts to run toward me, speeding up. I turn and leg it to the car. Just as I manage to drive out of the car park gate, he catches me up and slams both palms on the rear window. I accelerate along the lane, my heart galloping, reeling from the shock. I look into the rear-view mirror and he's just stood there, dressed in black with a balaclava on, motionless and intimidating.

I feel faint but hold it together until I reach a layby a few miles away and I pull the car in, under a tree, so it's not visible from the road. I lay my seat back and concentrate on my breathing. I try slowing it down, to stop the dizzy feeling that's putting spots in front of my eyes, moving me breath by breath to another blackout where The Whistler awaits. I manage to fool it by counting out loud and begin to come around. I'm shaking so I grab a blanket from the backseat and wrap it around me, like a shawl. The engine starts and blows warm air through the vents.

Making my way home slowly, I keep checking my mirror, in case I'm being followed. It dawns on me that the number of people I have left to call when I'm in a crisis are dwindling to a few who I am not sure I can trust. The thought makes me shudder.

I arrive at Lucinda's. The house is in complete darkness. It looks like a solemn face with blackened eyes, a nest with no chicks, a hollow place. It's so uninviting. I pop in, grab a few things, and head back to mine. It's time to face the music. Time to open old post and answer a myriad of sympathetic phone messages and deal with everything I've been running from. I guess life catches up with you eventually, ready or not.

The light is on in my hallway. I don't get out of the car. Someone's recently been through my rubbish bins. The contents are littered over the front lawn. Someone's been in the house. The door is ajar. I turn the car around and head for Karen's. It's the only place I can think of.

TWENTY ONE ~ The Asylum

I receive a call from Lucy on my second night at Karen's. She assures me she's OK and just needed a break. She's returned to her mother's. She's going to have the children there for a few weeks while she sorts herself out. Ewan is working with Anna on the plan with the Poles, so Karen and I decide to visit The Asylum. Tom is nowhere to be seen and I can't locate him. He isn't picking up calls. I've left numerous messages, telling him to go to my house if he needs a place to crash while he figures out his life. Anna won't answer my calls either. Karen went back to my house to check it over and found nothing out of place and nothing taken.

***

Our flight is noisy and rammed with people travelling home for the Christmas holidays. A subsequent lengthy car journey takes me on ascending narrow lanes, snaking around a maze of Scottish countryside. We seem to head inland. We don't pass through any villages or see signs for them, but head further into the foothills of a rocky, mountainous area. We end up not far from a place where a murmuring sea can be heard in the distance. Although we can't see it, the rolling mists and briny scent tell us we're near. The driver is silent the whole way and only occasionally flicks his eyes at us in the mirror. The sky is akin to something from a horror movie, dashes of monotonous steel-grey and stretches of purple-black cloud, with trailing wisps of white shifting quickly, as if blown by silent winds. It's an hour more before the driver suddenly stops at the gates of a ramshackle, Jacobean mansion and gets out our bags and dumps them at the roadside.

"You can't stop here. It's at least another mile to the door!"

"I'm sorry, miss, but I'm not taking my car up that lane. It's full of potholes."

He drives off in a hurry. Karen looks at me and shrugs her shoulders.

"We better get a move on. It's getting dark and it doesn't look like there are any B&B's around here either. Maybe they can book us one from inside."

She drags her suitcase behind her, looking more than a little unimpressed.

"Let's hope so, eh?"

"There aren't any lights on up at the house. That's weird. You don't think it's closed, do you? It looks very dark." Karen's laughter fades as we grow closer and the discernible darkness is more evident. The only sign of life is a nest of rooks in a crumbling chimney stack, a selection of ugly gargoyles peering down at us from under the eaves, and whatever wildlife might exist among the overgrowth of bushes and weeds that have completely taken over the grounds.

"Didn't you call ahead to say we were coming?" Karen asks.

"What do you think?" I say, taking in the blackened mansion. It's like a nebulous sketch, looming spires so tall they disappear into irrevocably dark mists. Heavily leaded, tall windows peer out into the fast approaching dusk, their glass, oil-black and lustrous. There is no sign to suggest this is Carton Hayes, but I feel it is. There is a story here, a presence. I sense it. Whispers of my past have been spoken here. A ghost of my ancestry has trodden these halls. I know some of my story lies within these mystical walls. The woman who knows about the beginning of my life who once wrote about me in letters, was in this very place. A woman who handed those letters to Ida, a nurse who then found them disturbing enough to track down my husband and tell him whatever she learned. The knowledge excites me, being here excites me, which is more than I can say for Karen.

"We need to call the taxi driver back here, or we'll

be stuck at this creepy old place all sodding night," Karen says, looking at her watch, then up to the fading daylight and sombre skies.

"I've haven't got any reception on my phone. You?"

"Me either."

"Rose, there's no way I'm going in there. It's similar to a bloody horror film set. It's probably not safe, either."

"We're going to need to get in. It's going to be dark soon and I don't see any other options, unless you want to bunk up with the hares and rats."

"Not funny."

We leave our suitcases on the steps and walk around the base of the building. We hug the stone wall until we come across a doorway, down a small flight of stairs, that's been boarded over. We manage to pry the rotting boards away easily and find ourselves in a long narrow corridor. It smells damp and faintly of cleaning chemicals. We walk along, kicking up sodden papers and critters scuttle out of our way. There's hardly any light, just enough to see a circular opening at the far end of the tunnel-like space. It's claustrophobic, finding our way along in the dark, with our hands exploring cold walls, and before long, our feet are soaked.

"I don't like this one bit. Why didn't you bloody well find out it was closed down? This is typical you, Rosie, everything's on a whim." She trips over a box and squeals.

"There's not a lot we can do about it now. Let's at least see if there's somewhere we can rest for a bit. It's too far to walk anywhere. We didn't pass any villages, not for over an hour. If we can get up to the top floor, we might have some signal."

"You're not saying that we're staying here for the night, Rose? I can't. I'd rather sleep outside."

"Be my guest," I say.

At the end of the corridor we find slate stairs that wind up through the building in a spiral fashion, similar to a fossil I found once at the beach. Beautiful carved balustrades, twisted like thick rope, are soft under our fingers as we climb four flights of stairs. The last of the violet daylight shines through the landing's stained-glass windows and guides us to the top floor. A row of empty glass-fronted offices echo our words as we speak, our voices bouncing off lofty ceilings. It's a drafty place, filling fast with all kinds of unexplainable shadows. Karen squeals at any new appearance or creak of the floorboards. The light disappears, and I rely on the torch from my phone to navigate us to a room that seems less airy and damp. A smaller office filled with filing cabinets and a couple of leather office swivel chairs.

There are stacks of old newspapers and magazines dotted about and the space smells acrid, of stale urine and disinfectant.

The strangest feeling floods in, a familiarity. I've been here before. I just know it. There's a curve of the ceiling in the room and an intricate, icing-white rosette with dancing angels and wreaths of holly. There is also a rancid odour that's permeated the walls.

"What's up? What are you looking at?" Karen asks, as I'm craning to see the last of the sun light up on the introverted dome ceiling.

"It's weird, but I think I've been here before."

"Maybe you have, perhaps when you were little. It wouldn't surprise me one bit." Her sudden contempt feels mildly threatening. She moves in and stands close to me, so I can feel the heat of her, while she whispers words into the back of my neck.

"You are a crazy bitch after all, eh, Rosie Love!"

"What are you saying? Stop being silly. This place is creepy enough without you acting up." I inch away, slowly, trying to gain a bit of distance as thin shadows flicker across the walls, while bats sky ride in search of insects outside. She called me Rosie Love. Rosie Love, Rosie Love… Did I tell her?

"Do you know that David wanted rid of you for years but feared what you might do to yourself? He only stayed with you out of pity." Her venomous words hit directly where they are intended, at my heart. For a second, breath escapes me. My mind races, trying to catch up with the reality of my new situation.

"I knew you always disliked me, but I never understood why. I never did anything to you, apart from love your brother." I'm nervous. I didn't see this coming.

"You really don't get it do you, how much he despised what you are. I never understood how he didn't see what everyone else saw." Her snigger is enough to make me step back until I'm against the wall.

"And what was that, Karen? What did they see? A broken kid from foster homes, that's all I was. I don't get your anger toward me. Was it jealousy?" Her laughter rings around the rafters, like a witch's cackle.

"No, you fucking moron. Not jealousy, hatred. I despised you. From the moment I saw those disgusting letters, I knew I was right about you, eh, mummy's little princess."

"So, you did lie? You knew what was in the letters."

"Everyone knew, me, David, Lucinda, Anna and my mum. We all knew. Why do you think we acted odd around you? Why do you think David didn't want kids with you? Ask yourself."

"That's bullshit. I couldn't have kids. I had tests. I know that he wanted kids. It broke his heart that we couldn't have a family. Anyway, the letters were recent."

"The tests were rigged, false. David had

connections. Why do you think he suggested his friend Dr. Becket, all the way down in London? The letters were given to David the year after he married you."

"Lies, all fucking lies!" I pick up the nearest instrument and launch myself from the wall so quickly that I catch myself by surprise. The length of broken piping comes down so hard that I hear a resounding crack as it meets with the top of Karen's skull. Jagged edges rip at her skin and snag her pretty auburn hair as I pull it away I give her a second blow to finish the job, shut the demented cow up once and for all. Blood spatters arc the walls and spray my face with warm iron-scented blood.

I feel nothing. She shakes and shivers, twitching, eyes wide. Her body moves and jerks, while her nerve ends dance around and battle dying. I've seen it on TV, but this is more exciting. I watch life leave her eyes. They glaze over, like frosted buttons. Her hair is slick with new blood. It smells like I imagine the first kill of a virgin hunter does. The act has awakened something evil. Was she right? Did I do something terrible before a time that I can remember? Why can't I remember? What is blocking out my childhood?

Bathed in bluish twilight, she looks ghoulishly pale and deathly wild. I close her eyes to stop her looking at me, as shadows continue to make ghostly shapes across the floor and the moon and earth rotate. I stay and watch, still and silent, until the first spot of sun lights her up, giving her a pinkish tint, humanising her once more. The blood is more vivid now. Dark pools of scarlet silk have gathered around her head. I wait until her skin is completely cold and takes on a waxy sheen, illuminated by the milky winter sun. Her veins at the temple are green as if mould is forming. Old cheese, Karen looks like old fucking cheese! My laughter is peculiar, raw somehow, strange, yet familiar. This place has divided me into a stranger from my illusive past and me from my obscure present, two halves of a deranged woman.

The walls know me. The floors feel me as I shuffle bare footed along corridor after corridor, taking in a nostalgic fetid stink of the place. The halls know me too. I feel a connection. There are stained glass windows everywhere I look, of saints and sinners that have an ethereal glow coming from behind them. I feel eyes of the past resting on me. How do I know this place?

Outside, once morning breaks streaking gold over the hills, my signal returns and I manage to get a taxi to come and pick me up.

Standing on the stairs, with my suitcase by my side, as if I'm leaving after a luxurious break in a mansion, waiting to leave, a thought hits me. It's cold and alarming, like precipitous rain on a windy day, a delayed discovery. I’m hit with the knowledge I've killed Karen, in cold blood. I've bludgeoned my prickly sister-in-law to death. My mind searches for logic, distress, emotion, but finds nothing but a reticent smile infused with joyous confusion and a longing to be home with Lucy and the girls. I've done it, ended a chapter I've waited to close for a long, long time.

I hide Karen's suitcase in among the nettles. I don't look back as we drive down the long, narrow lane. Never look back, you must never look back.

***

Home smells good. Recently purchased Christmas foliage scents the living room. Pine and wood smoke mingle as I crack open a bottle of red wine and get ready to settle in for the evening. This is my first night alone in my home for months, my first attempt at getting back to normal. I am putting the past in the past. Mowgli curls at my feet. The TV mutters on about all things joyous and Christmas cheer and glitzy entertainment programmes play out. Lucinda has promised to call in, to check on me, no doubt, to see if I'm coping, to see if I'm OK. Or is she calling by to ridicule our friendship with her barely hidden dishonesty. She knows my secrets, knows what's in the letters. Everyone but me knows, but I must not show her that I'm aware. I have to keep my composure, or she'll see right through me.

When I let her in, her smile seems so genuine, clever little liar. She's carrying a bag full of Christmas presents. The children are bubbling with excitement at her side.

"Merry Christmas!" They squeal in unison. I smile back.

"Same to you guys. Come on in. Let's go into the lounge, it's warmer in there."

They pile their coats on the kitchen table, revealing sickly festive jumpers, and kick their muddy boots off at the door. The kids run through and scatter my presents around the base of my sparsely decorated tree.

"Wow, I'm surprised to see a tree. Well done, you."

"It is Christmas, Lucy."

"With everything, you know it's a big step. Are you OK? You know you're welcome to come back to ours."

"I think I'll manage."

"How was Scotland? Did you find out any more about Isabelle's mum and the letters?" She looks shifty. She stares at the fire, flames dancing in her eyes, as she warms her hands, avoiding eye contact with me.

"Yes, as a matter of fact, I found out plenty."

"Anything you would like to share?" Her laughter is phony and her smile uncertain.

"No, it's not interesting, or important. Just some mad old woman and a few tales that made hardly any sense." I see a look of relief flicker in her eyes.

"So, you know, what the letters said?" she says, flaring angst from her pretty nose.

"Yep." Lucy has never been able to hide her feelings. She picks at her fingernails. The sound is discerning, irritating, a clicking, click, click, click.

"Lucy please, STOP IT!"

"Stop what? Is something the matter?"

"No, I'm just exhausted. It was a long and draining trip. And all for nothing, but the ramblings of an old woman that make no sense at all." By calling her bluff, I hope she might trip herself up and reveal to me that she knows what was in the letters.

"So, please tell me. What happened? What did you find out? It's still a fascination. Maybe, I can help. You know I enjoy a good puzzle."

"I'm glad you find this so amusing, Luce, but this is actually my life you're mocking."

"Hold on a minute, I'm not mocking. I'm trying to help you. Rose, did something happen up there between you and Karen that upset you?"

"No, we just had a few loose ends to tie up, things to talk through and we did. So, now it's on with my future. Look, I'm tired. I'm going to watch telly in bed. Do you mind if we catch up tomorrow?" The urge to get rid of her is overwhelming, an itch I'm desperate to scratch. Cunning bitch has been lying to me about those letters all these years. Was our entire friendship just a lie? I'm done faking smiles. Just looking at her smug face makes my insides churn.

"But the kids were so excited to spend time with you."

"I'll come over in the morning, like always, to see them open presents. I need to be alone. I've spent enough time leaning on you. I need to be able to stand on my own two feet for once." I hope she buys my friendly grin.

"You do talk nonsense, Rosie L... We're best mates. It doesn't even need saying. It's just something you do when you care about someone." She almost said it, Love. She knows alright.

"Do you care, I mean, really care?" I can't force my smile any longer.

"Rose, you're scaring me. That has to be the dumbest question I've ever heard. Of course I bloody do. Come here." Her arms curl around my neck and she steps in close, traces of Angel perfume in her hair. The feel of her, pressed against me, turns me rigid.

"Please, just go Lucy."

"Kids come on. We need to go."

"But Mum, we've only just got here." Sky says.

"Aunty Rose is tired. She'll be over in the morning, after Santa's been. Won't you?" I nod and squeeze the girls who are hanging off my legs and look up at me with huge innocent eyes.

Lucy glances back over her shoulder as she leaves and smiles, pink, glossy-lipped.

"See you tomorrow, get some rest. Love you, Buttercup." The words bring instant confusion. *Love you, Buttercup*. We always say it. But I can't say it back and as I close the door; emotion forces me to the ground. I want to believe, but Karen said, Karen, Karen… she said.

This time, as I begin to blackout, there is no pending darkness, only a blinding, celestial light. Once I'm there, transported to the place of dreams, it's cold. There's a malodorous smell, like faeces, that compels me to bring my hands over my mouth. I'm standing in a square room with a grey and white tiled floor. I'm naked, flea-bitten and scrawny. There is nothing in the room except for a mottled mirror on a dirty grey wall and a tiny hexagon-shaped window, too high to see out of. There are dark cracks running up the walls that stand out like veins on a long dead corpse. It's so intensely cold. My breath expels in small clouds. I pant, frightened. There's real fear, horrible deep-seated, anticipation.

Footsteps on hard ground grow louder. Not one set, but many. There are people. They're coming. A sinister whistling noise reaches me ahead of their arrival. It's loud and sad and terrifying, echoing as if there are multiple voices, whistling together, but out of sync, just enough to know it's a collective effort. A door I didn't notice starts to tremble as a key works the lock from the other side.

There are scrapes on my arm, not scratches, but long singular marks that stand out repulsively on my pallid skin. My temples throb and pain radiates through my limbs, like ants crawling, biting as they spread.

The door opens, and I see shadows, silhouettes of at least three people. The vision of them is shaky, as if I'm watching a digital glitch on a black and white TV programme. There are no faces, never faces. The people move as one and come toward me. I snap my head to the mirror., I’ve got short hair, cropped so close to my scalp I look like a convict, and my L-scar is pulsing, red and vulgar, as if it's alive. There are multiple thin lacerations to my shoulders. A hand that’s clammy and warm rests on my arm, it’s turns into an unfriendly grip. As I turn to meet my dream maker, I feel something warm on my face, brushing my cheeks over and over as if someone's painting my face with a brush of warm water. I close my eyes and let the sensation arouse me to wakefulness. Mowgli is licking my face and whimpering. I'm so glad to be awake that I hug him with all my might.

***

As light peeps from behind my curtains, and after a rotten night’s sleep, there's a loud thumping coming from my front door, an insistent bang that's not going to go away. I look out of the window and see Anna smacking it with her palms. Mowgli is barking, and I rush down to let her in.

"You'll wake the whole bloody neighbourhood with that racket."

"Where's Tom?"

"How would I know?"

"Since you were the last person to see him, I imagine you would know where he went."

"No, he didn't say. He left a note to say he was leaving. I've not heard from him since."

"Do you know what you've done with your meddling? Have you any fucking idea what you've started?"

"I think he deserved to know. We all deserve to know secrets that concern us. Isn't that so?"

"What right do you have? That is my business. Do you understand? I told you in confidence'" Her eyes are so close to mine that I can see my reflection. Heat from her breath reaches my lips and rage vibrates through her body as she fronts me; a warrior ready for battle.

"Letters, Anna. What was is those letters? Karen told me you all knew their contents. What was so shocking that you're all too scared to tell me?"

"I don't know what you mean. What bloody letters?" I'm confused. *She's telling the truth.*

"The letters David received from the old woman in The Asylum, just after we were married." I try again.

"I have no idea what Karen told you, but I have no idea about any letters. I'll call her now to clear this up. I just want to find out where my son is. I'm afraid he's going to do something stupid. That was so irresponsible, telling him like that."

"You can't call her. She's away," I say.

"Then it'll have to wait. Now, what exactly did you say to Tom? He's emptied his bank account and taken the rifle from the barn at the campsite. He's got a history of mental health issues. I swear, if any harm comes to my boy, I'm coming after you, you fucking lunatic. Now keep your nose out of my life. Stay the fuck away. Do… you… hear… me?" Her eyes are black, soulless, fathomless pits of hatred.

As the door slams shut and her car screeches out to the road, I wonder, was Karen actually telling me the truth? Or, was this just another of her spiteful games, to feed me enough rope to hang myself with? Did she really know about the letters? Is Lucy just my loyal friend, after all? The questions are tiresome, exhausting, ebbing and flowing like the tide. I contemplate the events of recent weeks in a warm bath and conclude that I should give Lucy one more chance to prove herself. After carefully choosing an outfit to cover my slightly scarred forearms, I make my way over to

Lucinda's with presents for the girls. It's the first time I've worn makeup since David died.

They're up, eating breakfast in the kitchen, when I arrive. The squeals are deafening as they run over to greet me.

"Father Christmas left these at my house for you," I say and hand them the boxes.

"Did I miss the main event?"

"No, we waited. Merry Xmas, Buttercup."

She hands me a coffee and a mince pie. We mosey into the lounge. The girls tear wrapping paper off a pile of presents. I know we're both thinking of David and how he loved these moments.

"You OK?" she asks.

"Not too bad, Lucy." I feel my face soften as we exchange sympathetic smiles.

The squeals continue and it's refreshing to witness genuine happiness. I'm able to put everything behind me and I relax into the day. The last few weeks have drained me and being here, right now, feels so comfortable, normal. The day unfolds into the most natural of family times. Lucinda is back to being attentive, caring. I forget about Karen and leave my knotted thoughts rotting in the past, in the mansion.

Christmas dinner is such a mouth-watering feast and we sit after on the floor with the kids, playing with their toys. we spend the afternoon cwtched (cuddled) in on the sofa; besties, watching festive films. I let everything go for today. I let it all go.

"You alright, Buttercup?" she asks, and I nod.

TWENTY TWO ~ Festive

New Year's Day starts with a bang. I wake to a message from Isabelle, saying she found another letter when she was going through her things. The only surviving letter that might shed some light on my past. She refuses to read it to me, assuring me that it's not what her mother would have wanted. As she was coming down this way to visit friends, she would drop the letter in. The news is overwhelming. At last, a verification of sorts, that I existed as a child. No matter how horrible it might be, and I do know there'll be information I'm not happy about. There's been a feeling of dread that I've carried with me all these years, just lurking in the background, behind fortress doors. I need to know what lies beyond. I was informed as a teenager that my mother was too ill to look after me and was in a residential home. She wouldn't know me if I looked her in the face, so I presume it may have something to do with my father, another mystery. There's a human being, a life, a personality whose genes I carry. Could this mysterious past lie with him?

"Penny for your thoughts," Lucinda says, breaking me from my thoughts.

"Oh, don't mind me, dreamer. I always did have my head in the clouds."

"Yes, remember, in history lessons, when you used to doodle in your scrapbook. One time you ended up getting the cane for drawing angel's wings."

"Yes, I'd forgotten about that. Mrs. Jones was good at cracking her whip. I can still hear the sound of it, nasty old cow."

"So, are you going to tell me what you were thinking about?"

"Why not? I was thinking about Isabelle. She text to say she found a letter in her mother's things, when she was packing away her house. It's the only letter left from the woman in The Asylum. This could be the key to my past."

"Are you sure that's what you want? It seems whatever was in those letters sent people around the bend. Sometimes, the mystery can out way the grimness of the reality."

"You sound as if you don't want me to read it?"

"I'm just saying, there's no going back. Whatever secrets were authored by that mad woman, they seem to spell bad news."

"I know it's not going to be bedtime reading, but I'm ready to know."

"Well if you're sure, but just don't get too down heartened if there's upsetting news. After all, a woman in an asylum was writing letters to a nurse about things that concern you. I really can't imagine what the story is there. What if it's to do with your parents? What if they did something terrible? Just think about all the secrets you've unravelled since David died. Do you really need more to add to the collection?"

"I need to have a life that's blemish free, no secrets, mysteries or unanswered questions. However bad the news is, it's got to be better than not knowing, guessing bad things, horrendous things, day after day. How can I ever move on if I don't know where I come from? Seven years of my life, my formative years and I don't know how they were. What was my life was like? Who was around me? Was I a happy little girl?"

"OK, I get that, I really do. I'm just saying, brace yourself for a fall. Because if David knew about those letters and chose not to tell you, it would have been to protect you from something."

"It's high time I found out what that something is. She'll be here tomorrow afternoon." Lucinda alters her face, the way she does when about to change the subject.

"Why don't we go for a swim this afternoon? I fancy a bit of exercise. Come on, it will be fun."

"OK, I'm up for that."

The pool is empty save for a lifeguard sat on a high post, looking bored. He is probably pissed off he got the short straw for having to work during the holidays.

The water is still. It sends increasing ripples across the pool when we slip in. We cling to the sides, doing a few kicks and stretches to warm up.

"Just so you know, I don't want to meet Isabelle," Lucinda says, rather abruptly.

"That's possibly the weirdest thing I've heard you say. What reason could you possibly have to not want to see her?"

"No reason, I just think you should do this part alone. I'll be there if you need me, but I think you should meet just the two of you."

I leave it there, but the suggestion that she doesn't want to meet Isabelle bugs me all day. We swim fifty lengths, thrashing them out, competitively, then cycle home, racing one another.

There's a feeling edging back in, a natural sarcasm we've fallen into, a melodramatic rhythm, that's been there all our lives, subtle enough to be considered banter, but just enough to make the jokey jibes hurt a little.

It seems to be a pattern. We bond and enjoy a certain amount of time together that then becomes suffocating. Then we bicker and need a break. I'm glad to be living at mine but visiting her. That way I can break away if I feel we're getting too argumentative.

"Why don't you ask Karen if she'll go with you to meet Isabelle. She must be interested after visiting The Asylum with you."

"No, I think you're right. I'd rather to meet her alone. She seemed nice. You'd like her. She's a bit of a hippy, but there's something serene about her. You know, one of these women totally happy in their own skin."

"Wow, you got a lot from one visit. Is she attractive?"

"Yes, in a natural kind of way. Rosy-cheeked, but dark glossy hair. I'd say one of her parents is oriental. She's easy to talk to. I can see why she and David were friends." Lucinda straightens her face and slams her coffee cup on the kitchen table.

"What was that for?" Her mini temper tantrum amuses me.

"Nothing, I'm being a dick, ignore me. I'm uptight lately, still have issues with, you know."

"It will get better as time goes on. It's never easy dealing with death," I say, feeling helpless to make her feel better.

"I say we take the kids down to the beach for a run out with the dog. Fresh air is such a tonic when you're fed up. What do you say?" She nods her agreement and we bundle the kids into the car.

We're half away across the beach when the heavens

open. Hard, driving rain pummels us as we begin to sprint in the sand, the kids screaming with excitement and fear. Lucy scoops up Sky and Summer grabs my slippery hand as we continue to run towards the car park. By the time we've reached the car, we're soaked to the bone, wet clothes sticking to our skin. We quickly take off our outer layers and place them in the boot where the dog curls into his bed. Lucinda starts the engine and blows warm air through the vents. After a few minutes, the windows steam up. The rain continues to assault the car from all angles. The car warms up quickly and we drink hot tea from a flask. It's like being inside a tent, the windows frosted over from warm breath and hot air. There's no visibility outside, just the sound of the rain hammering the roof and the kid's giggles. Mowgli's soft snores come from the boot.

I decide to make a face in the steam to entertain the kids while Lucy dries them off. I begin by drawing an eye.

"It's moving," squeals Sky from the back seat. Lucy grabs hold of my arm. There's movement behind it, a flicker.

I quickly rub at the window screen to reveal a man dressed head to toe in black, standing in front of the car. The rain is obscuring his face. He's a well built man, the same man as before?

"Lucy let's get out of here, quickly," I say quietly so

I don’t scare the kids. She puts the car in reverse and we move, but the man just stands there, not moving a muscle, watching as we accelerate out of the car park. That chilling sight troubles us both, just the same as the day Tom knocked me down on the beach. Again, we don’t say much, especially as we don’t want to alarm the girls, but there is an undertone of panic lodged in my throat and Lucy's hands are trembling. *Who is following me?* It has to be Old Man Jenkins or one of his thuggish cronies. He must know I've blabbed to Tom. He’ll be livid, dirty old pervert, seething, angry. The thought of his angry pandemonium satisfies me greatly. It's a good result. I imagine that Ewan and Anna are having to speed things up with the Poles because of my meddling, but I don't care. The quicker that man is out of the picture, the better.

***

Isabelle is due to call any minute and the house is gleaming. It's the first excuse I've had to give the place a good clean, an airing. There’s a strange form of catharsis to wiping away the grime. With the cleaning comes a feeling of mind de-cluttering, like I’m emptying out my mind’s accumulated chaos. David and Karen’s deaths are washed away with a few scourers and some elbow grease. It's the clearest of mind I’ve felt in some time. Sitting in my lemon-scented kitchen, in my home, I’m quite alone but for once, not lonely.

The phone ringing takes me out of my Doris Day moment. Tom's voice is a welcome relief.

"Hey, it's me." He sounds dismal.

"Your mum's been worried sick. You should call her."

"I can't face her at the minute. It's all too much. But you can let her know I'm safe, please. I'm staying with friends in Aberystwyth."

"Ok, I'll let her know. Don't leave it too long. She needs you."

"I have things to sort before I can tackle my oddball family. Anyway, that's not why I called. I was at the beach the other day, just staring at the sea, feeling, you know, at one with it. I know this might sound crazy, but I was thinking about how similar we are. Stormy one minute, dragging muck up from the depths, and then calm, glittered and warmed by the sun, and the storm is forgotten. Thinking about storms, I recalled a conversation I overheard with my grandad a few years ago. I don't know if it's relevant to my situation now. Him and Mum were arguing. It was bad. He said something about me having an older brother that died. His name was Seth Jenkins. I'm guessing he would have been around forty now. I'm wondering, could he have been another product of my grandads, you know...?"

"Wow, Tom, that's big news. I guess you'll just have

to ask him, or your mum, when you're ready. Life can get ugly sometimes. I'm sorry, so sorry I opened such a tragic door for you." His silence says everything, and the phone's ending click makes me shudder and pray his mum wasn't right about him doing something stupid.

The doorbell chimes out a cheerful tune and Isabelle's silhouette from behind the glass reminds me of the Queen's head on a penny.

She comes in carrying the fresh air on her clothes and hair and a soapy scent to her skin. She's warm and friendly, hugging me as if we're lifelong mates. We sit at the kitchen table with a perfunctory plate of biscuits in front of us, to eat with our cups of tea. She hands me the letter. Silence falls around us as I flip open the leaf and slide the scented paper out of the envelope. My heart flutters in my chest. A flush blooms on my cheeks as anticipation overcomes me. I unfold the letter. The writing's beautifully slanted, almost italic. I'm almost afraid to read it.

Dearest,

Thank you for your last letter.

I think I told you before that for a little one to have to have kept such sad secrets would have been a pressure too much. I don't think that it would have helped her in any way to have a happy and normal life. She must

never know. Whatever happened all those years ago, the incident must die with you and I.
You've been a lifeline and my gratitude for all those years of listening to me unburdening my story, I know is not repayable. I wouldn't know how. I'm so glad that during your working life, here at the 'nut house,' you gravitated toward me. And more importantly, you didn't treat me like one of the circus freaks they keep locked away in here. Thanks to you and your kindness and perseverance, my life here has been ordinary and as bearable as can be expected.
I'm so very sad about your news, sad that my only connection to the outside world is about to end. I hope you suffer no pain, my dear friend. As for that poor little might, Rosie Love, let her story die with you. Please, I beg you. What happened to her must be forgotten with us. Burn the letters.
Warmest Wishes,
Mary

"You OK?" Her eyes search my face as I try to make sense of the letter.

"Yes, I think so. It's an odd letter, but it confirms my name is indeed, Rosie Love. Whoever this woman was, she had confided my entire story to your mum. I think the truth died with them both. I don't think I'll ever know now. David's gone. Your mum's gone too and this woman, Mary, there's no record of her after The Asylum closed down, as if she just vanished. I presume she's dead too. This Mary woman must have known my family somehow. I've known for a long time that my real mum's been in a home for years with dementia. I don't know why I felt compelled for this to be a secret. She doesn't recognise anyone, so I'm told, so that's a dead end. I never knew my dad. I guess I'll never know my true story. Maybe this is a sign I should stop looking. Did your mum ever give you a hint of anything that she gleaned from the letters?"

"No, I'm sorry. She was a stickler for loyalty. She kept a promise to this woman and maintained it to her deathbed. It's always bothered me that she confided in David though, and not me. I never worked out why. Maybe, she needed whatever protection they had for you, to be carried on after her death. She wasn't to know David would die; I suppose."

We have a few quiet moments and awkward pauses before Isabelle heads off, on her way. Out of loyalty to her mum, she declined my offer to read the letter. I wave her off and a sudden calm wash through me. There is a sense of this being the end of the road, as far as my murky past is concerned. There's no way of knowing the truth and I'm surprised at my lack of disappointment.

The box from Margery's attic catches my eye and I

absentmindedly flip open the lid. I think maybe I should burn these letters too. They're just paper after all. What good could come from them now? I pick up a pile of them and the garish ring drops onto the table and spins before it settles. Light from the lamp glints on the initials engraved on the inside: SJ. Seeing them sparkle, sparks a memory, something said in the conversation to Tom earlier. The name, Seth Jenkins. SJ.

It's as if a burning sensation, raw and swift, is sweeping through me, like flames rising in a forest fire. When clarity comes, it's akin to a perfect, clear sky after a long storm. There's an overwhelming urge to do something drastic, run into the sea, or scream, or cut my wrists just a little to relieve the pressure of euphoria versus pain. The truth. Finally.

Seth Jenkins is David's real name. He was Tom's older brother. Anna's first bastard son. Another child born from rape. The anonymous letter to Margery was from Anna. I think of how young she must have been, how terrified, but how selfless, to give up her child, to watch him being carried away, crouching in foliage at the edge of the woods. My God, that's why she was at David's funeral. He was her son.

At last, a reason for Old Man Jenkins to hate me. I had the love of his first born, bastard son. He must have found out. That's why he killed Margery. The reality is breath-taking, an unexpected twist that makes perfect sense.

I'm engulfed by sadness for the entire situation. My heart physically aches for the pain suffered at the hands of that man. The world spins and spins and I need Lucy. I need to hear her voice. I need my oldest, best friend to make the world right.

TWENTY THREE ~ Lucinda

Lucinda is at the park, sat on a viewing bench, while the girls run up to the top of the slide and come down backwards. The sound of their laughter is refreshing and tinkles into a clear blue morning. She doesn't know I'm watching them all until Sky shouts, "Auntie Rosie, watch this…" And off she flies backwards, squealing, with Summer behind her, on her belly, holding onto her sister's ankles.

"How long have you been standing there?" Lucy says.

"Not long," I say, quietly.

"Remember how happy we were as kids, Rose?"

"How could I forget? I recall you wouldn't let me be sad. You kept me too busy, made me smile before I had a chance to even frown. I'm lucky to have you as a friend."

"I take it she's been?"

"If you mean Isabelle, yes, but I didn't get the answers I thought I would from the letter. It was just another road to yet another dead end."

“What did the letter say?”

“A woman called Mary, who was a patient at The Asylum was writing to a nurse who cared for her, Isabelle’s mum, Ida. It seems she confided things to her about my childhood, an incident from my lost years, things that have gone to the grave. I'm afraid it was just a goodbye letter with hints of a mysterious past. Or, the ramblings of an old lonely lady, who knows. Maybe she was crazy. I did, however, just find something else out that's surreal. I've not quite got my head around it all yet.”

“About your past?”

“About all of ours, David's mostly.” Her eyes light up.

“This is really hard to explain, Lucy, and promise you won't get mad. Remember when Margery died, and I cleared out her house with Karen?”

“Yes.”

“There's something I didn't tell you about that day.”

“Go on…”

“I found a box in the attic containing letters. They proved David was adopted.”

“You are shitting me, right? You don't remember telling me this before?” I rack my brains trying to remember such a conversation.

“No, I'm sure I didn't and that's not all. There was a ring amongst the papers, an ugly, garish, men’s gold ring with the initials SJ engraved on the inside."

"I found out from Tom just now. He overheard Anna and his grandad arguing over an older brother that supposedly died over forty years ago. His name was Seth Jenkins. Brace yourself, this part is awful and difficult to say. Old Man Jenkins raped Anna, his own daughter. The abuse started not long after his wife died, when Anna was still so, so young." I surprise myself being overcome with emotion at saying the words aloud. Lucy's hand clamps over her mouth, but her bulging eyes convey her disbelief and shock.

"Rose, your memory worries me. You told me David was adopted, but this, about Anna, it's all so tragic."

"Tom is his son too and a there's a disabled daughter. I think David is Anna's first-born son." I have no recollection of our conversation; it seems I can't even trust my own mind. Lucy looks punch drunk, like I've just whacked her with a cricket bat, dazed, wilting, about to flop to the floor.

"Whoa, Rose, that's some really heavy information to take in, like it's seriously ludicrous. Are you certain?"

"I'm ninety-nine percent sure, but Anna doesn't know I've connected all the dots yet. I want to go and see her. I need to hear the full story from the horse's mouth. It's going to be a very emotional conversation for us both."

“How did you find out that she was abused by the old man?”

“She told me, last time I saw her.” Lucinda’s whole demeanour deflates. Her shoulders drop. Her arms dangle loosely at her sides and her face sags.

“What a disgusting bastard. why did she stay around him? I mean, it's sick to even think about it.”

“She was afraid of him and, of course, Tom didn't know until recently. He had control over the businesses too. I guess she was trapped.”

“Poor kid, can you imagine how stomach-churning that must be? I can't believe you kept all this from me. We've never had secrets, Rose. I've gotta say, I'm a little disappointed you didn't tell me sooner. You see me almost every day.” Her eyes flash with disappointment, but something else too, sorrow.

“You’ve had a lot to deal with recently, with that poor boy hanging himself.... I didn't want to bother you with more drama.”

“It's been a harrowing year for us both. Will you let me come when you go to see Anna?” I don't answer immediately because I'm not sure I want her to come. I've liked the independence I've found in recent weeks, away from us, the confines of our friendship.

“I'll let you know when I think about going, OK?” This seems to pacify her, for now. My mind is desperately searching for a memory of the conversation about David being adopted, but I can't find it. Tricks, mine or hers?

***

I end up at Burry Port, sat in my car, facing rows of yachts with pretty names, and tired looking fishing boats tilting to one side in lustrous silt, awaiting buoyancy from a surge of water to bring them upright. The moon tide comes quick and fast, carrying with it distant noises from across the estuary, giving me time to think. Although my house is not such a tragic place to go to anymore, it is still empty. The murmurs of quiet as I rattle around in it, like a loose coin in a pocket, amplify my loneliness and being alone, outside, watching life happen, feels somehow less lonely. The smallest of things, I find pleasing, like the car full of teenagers, windows down, music pouring out. A man walking his old, fat Labrador, smoking a cigarette or a paper bag blowing across the carpark, scratching at the concrete or a young couple necking on a bench, hands exploring, oblivious to who's watching. It's good to be a witness to these small things. I notice everything. I'm interested in the small snippets of life no one else notices or cares about. I get the importance of it all.

A few more days at home by myself is just what the doctor ordered. There will always be a trace of David in every part of our home. I no longer wish to eradicate him, his memory, I wish to live comfortably, knowing he's not really gone. I can deal with the thought he's away on a permanent business trip. And it's OK to hate him sometimes. After all, I buried ashes that might not have been his. If it wasn't for the car hired in his name and some random contents from his suitcase, flung from the window, there would be no actual confirmation the remains were his. So, I choose to believe he's alive. At least while I'm here in our space.

Lucinda asks me daily when we are going to see Anna. I'm failing as a friend, not responding to her voice messages. I'm ignoring her, putting her in the back of the closet, like an overused toy I've tired of. The more time I spend alone in my house, the more I like myself. It's invigorating. I'm consumed with confidence. Every day I accumulate strength by her absence alone.

Today I feel ready to go and thrash it out with Anna. I also intend to put a halt to the naysayers once and for all. I will rid myself of the negativity, get myself some light therapy and let them know, it's out there. The secret has exploded out right of the bag. It's going to be painful, but it will be another chapter concluded. I have to be resilient and remember this is about me. Today is about *my* counterfeit smile.

Anna agrees to meet me at the lake. I recall speaking to Karen in the very same spot Anna awaits me now.

Tall, burnt-orange grasses rustle at the water's edge

in the cool breeze. The vivid autumnal colour lingering after a mild winter. Teal water is dappled and laps gently not far from our seat. She hears me approach and turns.

"I trust you want to talk about Tom?" She looks like a spy from a movie, her blonde bob neatly wrapped in a chiffon scarf, large black sunglasses perched on her nose, red lips, full, perfect.

"Yes, I thought it was time we talked, but not about Tom."

"What then. Don't you think you've done enough damage to my family?"

"The damage wasn't done by me though, was it?"

"You are full of riddles, Rose. Can't you just say what you bloody well mean?"

"Where's the fun in that? I thought you enjoyed guessing games, giving people the run around."

"Please, I don't have time for this." She gets up to leave and I tug at her coat sleeve.

"OK, I'm sorry. I know what you've been through. I just found out something that makes your business mine and it's not easy."

The way her head leans, slightly to the side, and how she removes her sunglasses, slowly to show me the serious depths to her dark blue eyes, makes me reconsider my abrupt delivery. I try a more tactful approach.

"I know about David. It's over Anna. I know he was your son."

She looks flabbergasted, grief-stricken. I give her time to compose herself. Her hands fiddle with the clasp on her handbag. Her eyes remain fixed on the subtle movement of the water. After a long silence, she speaks first.

"How did you find out?"

"Tom. He overheard an argument, a long time ago, you and your dad talking about his older dead brother Seth. He put two and two together, I guess. I also found your letter and the ring at Margery's." Her face crumples as her memory and reality collide and her words are merely a whisper to herself.

"He knew, my poor boy."

"Yes, he must have stored the words away until they made sense."

"I never wanted Tom to know the truth. Seth was so little, so perfect. I wanted a better life for him, away from all the violence and sickness."

"What about Tom and Nini? Why did you keep them in such a hostile environment?"

"Because it all stopped after Tom was born. Suddenly everything changed. He started to be fatherlier, less intrusive. He got old, moved into the annex and made sure he was just a grandad to the kids. I felt we were all out of danger. He gave me the businesses to run, like a payment to keep my mouth shut, and nothing was ever spoken of again." There is a look of shame she can't disguise, no matter how much expensive lipstick and perfume she uses to mask the dirt. It's etched into the deep worry lines under her eyes.

"You know, Rose, this isn't your problem. David didn't know the truth. My dad found a letter I had written to give to Margery. I was going to ask to contact Seth, or David. He went ballistic, said he would kill David, if David ever found out the truth. But he went and somehow introduced himself, started business dealings with him, brought him into our home. It was just fantastic to have him around. My dad was fascinated with his new, clever son. David was oblivious. But after a while, he found out David was stealing from him. It was huge amounts of money. His fascination turned to obsession, then hatred. I'd never seen my father so wild-eyed and crazy before. He started following him, telling me about you, how he would target you too because anything connected to David was filth. His anger was this uncontrollable rage that kept on snowballing until he couldn't see straight. He watched his every move. Betrayal is my father's worst fear and in some sick way, because he was his son, even though David didn't know, he saw the deceit as unforgivable. He was Hell-bent on making him pay, somehow."

"Do you think he killed David?"

"I have my suspicions. I wouldn't put anything past him, but I could never prove anything. When you came asking questions, I panicked. That's why I was so horrible. I thought if I made you go away, you'd be safe. Ewan was already helping me plan to get my dad out of the way. That abhorrent animal deserves everything he's got coming to him."

The whole facade is earth shattering, darkly poetic, but there's also a quiet relief in all this madness. One more chapter is closing. To know the truth brings serenity.

When I arrive home, the answerphone is flashing red and there are fifteen missed calls from Lucinda, who's also texted me.

"Call me, it's urgent!"

Her phone rings out and eventually, after what seems like an age, Sky answers.

"Mummy's busy. Can I take a message?"

"Sky, it's Aunty Rose. Where's Mummy?"

"She's talking to the policeman."

"OK, tell her I'm on my way." My mind goes straight to the bad and, also, back to almost a year ago, when I sat facing two policemen, listening to them tell me my husband was dead.

There are two police cars on her drive and neighbouring curtains are twitching at a speed of great nosiness. Lucinda waves me over.

"Rose, come and sit down. There's been some awful news."

I see the scrunched-up note paper with Lucinda's address on it, in the policeman's hand. I had written it out for Tom, with the home telephone number, so he could keep in touch. But he had taken it with him. My stomach tightens as the beginnings of macabre news starts to bleed poison. *Tom, poor Tom.*

"Anna's been in an accident. They found my address in her car, on this piece of paper, and came to inform us." She takes the paper and pushes it across the table to me. I blink so hard I can almost hear it, like shutters on a camera. *Anna, not Tom.*

"Inform us of what, exactly?"

"She was run off the M4 by a lorry. Her car went into the central reservation. Rose, I'm sorry. She didn't survive." Lucinda doesn't take her eyes off of my face.

I hold onto the kitchen worktop to steady myself. I stop hearing words and just see faces, sliding around like smudges on a dirty glass. I picture Anna's headscarf like a bandage, blood seeping through. I find myself on the floor in the dark, wailing, fighting for breath. My heart is beating fast, then, skipping beats. My chest is tighter than a drum, hurting, wanting to escape the confines of my chest.

I hear whistling, *Melancholia*, it's such a sinister

tune. The footsteps are loud and as quick as a train, galloping along the tracks. The door handle to my dark room rattles. I'm small, so, so small, terrified. He's coming for me and his presence is monstrous, demonic. I open my mouth to scream as the door creaks open, letting in shards of dull light, and his shadow fills the room. A large hand pushes into the darkness. He's never gotten this close before. His fingertips are almost on my nose. My screams wake me.

"Rosie, it's OK. I'm here. I'm never going to leave you. You are safe. Just breathe."

I come around on her dog-eared corduroy sofa. The policemen are gone. Perhaps it was a dream?

"Anna?" I ask, but she shakes her head and I begin the nightmare of hearing the news all over again. I can't get Tom out of my head. What will this do to him? Is the young girl, Nini, safe? Old Man Jenkins did this. I'm convinced. He's ensuring his dirty secret remains hidden. How far will he go to protect the secret of his incestrial brood? I'm guessing all the way, which puts me in danger too. I suggest that now might be a good time for that trip to Porthcawl.

***

The impromptu trip has stirred up all kinds of logistical problems. The kids can't come out of school as term's started. Lucinda is in the middle of an important case and can't leave work. I suggest that I go on ahead and she come at the weekend with the kids.

I book into a hotel on the seafront using an anonymous name. Anna is in my thoughts all the time. The image of her turning to me from the bench as I arrived at the lake plays over and over in my mind, her red-lipped smile. What a horrific and untimely death. After all her years of silent suffering. She will remain an eternal heroine in a gloomy play, only with no happy ending. What a grisly end, on a motorway, on a stormy afternoon.

I'm certain Old Men Jenkins will come for me. I've no doubt. I've feared nothing in my life, except for the macabre thoughts I cannot find, but that withered old man terrifies me.

The rear-view mirror is turned toward me. I check it all the time, glancing around me. My shoulders are bunched and there's no chance of me relaxing. I fear for Tom, too. Is he safe now the truth's out? Is Lucinda safe? I imagine that now I've rocked the boat; the old man will be simmering with malice. All the evil that he'd managed to suppress after the birth of Tom is now bubbling to the surface and is about to boil over in a frenzied car crash.

The hotel is a seventies shambles inside, a mock Victorian mess. Dark, blood-red carpets and clunky, dark wood furniture clutters the hallway. Gold-framed pictures of hunting scenes cover the walls and heavy, scarlet, velvet curtains and drapes block out most of the natural daylight. There's a claustrophobic feel to the place and there's a lingering scent of furniture polish. The man behind the reception desk looks like he belongs in black and white movie. A cumbersome lump in pinstripes and braces, with a neatly combed Majors moustache. He's jolly, in a rouge-cheek kind of way, and asks me to fill out a lengthy form with my details. I give a false name and tell him I'm expecting guests tomorrow and book a room for Lucy and the girls under a pseudonym.

My room's light and airy. Lofty ceilings are full of small cracks, similar to glazed pottery. The space is peaceful and minimalistic, decorated in whites and pale blues. Delicate, voile curtains flutter in a briny, sea breeze from an open window. It's such a contrast to the theatrical downstairs. I could be in a different hotel altogether.

After unpacking my things, I decide to take a bath and turn the taps to fill the tub. The bathroom fills with steam and I discard my clothes into a messy pile on the white tiles. As the water gushes, I try to ignore the throbbing at my temples the noise that it brings and massage it away with my fingertips, as David used to do when I had a migraine. I glance in the mirror and smile at my frown. I notice my lines are becoming more and more deep. I swipe away a veil of mist from the mirror and to my horror, the reflection staring back isn't mine.

My pulse quickens until I hear it in deafening whooshes. My heart gallops and I hold my breath, rigid with terror. A young woman with a bloodied and beaten face, looking petrified and desperate, stares back at me. Her eyes are so haunting, so sad, she's pleading to me for help. Her mouth is open. She's screaming, but there's no sound. I close my eyes to shake away the vision, but she remains, silently screaming, begging, hands ripping out clumps of hair in frustration. I sprint to the bed and duck under the covers like a child afraid of the dark. *It's a vision, just a vision. It's not real.*

I stay under the covers while my heartbeat slows and returns to a normal rhythm and a wave of exhaustion sweeps me faraway, into a beckoning, deep, deep, sleep.

By the time Lucy arrives, two days later, I haven't left the room. The bath remains full. I'm afraid to look in the bathroom mirror. She's left the girls with her mum, claiming they didn't want to miss a school dance. I can see she's dismayed at the state of me, hair uncombed. I must reek of sweat. I've slept on and off, dreaming the most peculiar dream; me cowering in the corner of a room, covering my ears to block out distant screams. I tell Lucy this. She says I need to take a tablet and get some fresh air. She sits on the side of the refilled hot bath and shampoos my hair. She convinces me to take a walk along the promenade.

It's cold. There are hardly any people around. It's sobering and tranquil. We link arms and walk for miles. I'm so grateful for her gentle touch and words of wisdom.

"We need to get you something to eat. You have to start looking after yourself. You don't eat enough." Her voice is mellow and warm, but, ever so slightly, motherly.

"I will. I promise. Do you think I'm losing my mind, Lucy?"

"No, you lost your marbles years ago," she says, laughing, teasing, always teasing. I think she's teasing. Is she?

We eat at a small cafe and sit in a window seat looking out as a grey mist rolls in.

"Rose, I've been meaning to ask you, do you think it's best if you sell up and move in with me and the girls, permanently?"

"Just because I've had a few scares, doesn't mean I'm not capable of looking after myself," I say, defensively.

"That wasn't what I meant. It would be really nice to have you there; the girls love having you around and I do too. It feels like a proper family when your home. You could free up some money and take it easy, go on a holiday to forget, get away from all this tragedy." It makes sense. Maybe, it would be good. I thought I was coping OK, until here, in this strange hotel.

"Rose, think about it. You've had a run of bad news and bad luck. You've not reacted well to any of it. When I first met you, all those years ago, you were still having the occasional meltdown, blackouts. You've spent years getting away from your past. Why are you so Hell-bent on letting it catch up with you? I know that what happened to David was a shock. It was to all of us. But looking back is never a good thing to do, especially in your case. A fresh start is what you need, with people around you that care. We could even take the girls and move away, somewhere new."

"That sounds dreamy, but it's not the past catching up with me Lucy. It's always there, pecking at my brain. I was a person, living somewhere. My identity feels fake, like I've had to make it up as I go along. When you have no past to cling onto, you are forever in limbo, hanging in mid-air, waiting to be claimed by your memories. It's hard to explain. but I feel alone, as if it's always been just me. no matter how many people are around."

"As long as I'm around, you'll never be alone. I'll always be here for you. Haven't I always been there, Rose?"

The question brings about an old faded memory.

We are sitting on the edge of the lake and then decide to take a swim. We're young, early teens. She is pulling me out of the water, after my legs became tangled up in the reed beds and I almost drowned.

"I'm here, Rosie. You nearly bloody drowned. It's a good job I was here. It's Ok now. I'll always be here for you, Rose." Her big brown eyes were glinting in the sun and I remember feeling so grateful. I look at her now, her eyes sparkling, like they did then, with love and adoration.

"Maybe we should move in together?" I say. She winks at me and blows the froth from her latte at me and it lands on the table. She moves it around with her finger and looks up at me, eyes wide. Her phone is buzzing in her bag.

"Are you going to get that?" I ask. But she ignores my question and continues to prod at the froth.

"Lucy, the phone," I insist, but she reaches into her bag and switches it off.

"It's probably Mum, checking I got here OK," she says.

"So, why didn't you answer? She'll be worried. You know what she's like." She looks uncomfortable and absent-mindedly places her hands over her handbag, as if to protect it. I leave it there but decide to wait until we are back at the hotel to have a look to see who called. She fidgets in her chair and a flush comes over her face.

"You OK, Lucy? You look like something's wrong."

"I'm fine, a little stuffed from all this food." She pushes her plate of sandwich crusts away.

"Let's make our way back. We can have a nice glass of wine and watch a film in the room and plan what we're going to do tomorrow," she says, looking more cheerful, as if whatever fleeting thought made her fret has left.

"Do you think Old Man Jenkins is a threat? Do you think he'll come after me, us?"

"No, listen to me, Rose. You have to stop with the paranoia. The police interviewed the lorry driver. It was a genuine accident. Think about it, he loved his family. He might have been an evil man, but I seriously doubt he would want to harm them. He's probably too devastated to even contemplate anything that horrible. I don't think you will hear from him or Tom again."

Her words tumble around, over and over, as we amble back to the hotel. By the time we get into the warm and settle on the bed with wine and chocolate, I've concluded that we're safe and that it's time to let it all go and move on.

Lucy goes to the bathroom mid-film and I spy her handbag hanging off the back of the chair. I tiptoe over and slip my hand in and pull out her phone. Only it's not her phone. It's the bat phone. The room seems to shrink around me. I don't know what to do with it and I'm still thinking, thinking, thinking when Lucy appears from the bathroom, drying her hands on a tissue. She sees I'm in shock and says, "Give me the phone, Rose." Her face is unreadable.

"Why do you have it? It was in my bedside drawer. How did you get it?"

"This one is a different one. The one you have was Summer's, this one's Sky's." I turn it over and read: '*Daddies bat phone*' on the sticker, but this sticker is blue, not pink.

My head is racing ahead, but it's not coming up with a logical explanation.

"Are you telling me what I think you are?"

I read a text and wind leaves my sails. I'm not sure whether to be furious or to collapse on the bed. I'm not sure of anything at all. The text on the bat phone reads,

'Daddy I miss you x'

My heart stops. *No, please, no, not this.*

TWENTY FOUR ~ Tragedy

Lucy fidgets and picks at her fingernails, the way she does when she's nervous. I didn't know it was possible to love and despise someone at the same time. How do you do it, turn a lifetime of love into hatred? I can't speak, but I observe her compulsion to do things with her hands to keep them busy, and the slight twitch in her upper lip. That's the thing, when you know someone so well. These small signs of distress signify stress and worry. Her eyes are watery, filled with genuine remorse, but how can I forgive her? I enter our conversation knowing I'm going to come out of it completely alone.

"The bat phone's, are they're really yours?" My words are difficult to say, but I manage them confidently. She doesn't answer. Her eyes do the talking and she makes a simple, choking sound.

"Are both of the girls his?"

"Yes." It's barely audible. Tears come now, making tracks down her cheeks. There's no point wiping them away because she knows there'll be more.

"I'm so sorry. Will you let me explain?"

My stomach tightens and my mind lurches. I run to the window and throw it open, gasping for air, taking it deep, deep inside. The day looks broken, the world all askew. My life is one huge lie.

I can't look at her, so I ask while facing the sea, "Were you in love?"

"He loved us both equally. You have to believe that. I love you too, more than I ever did him, always have."

"Do you know how sick that sounds?" I wait for my anger to surge but strangely, it doesn't. "Fuck Lucinda, you could have had anyone. Why him, after everything you knew about me, why?"

I feel considerably composed, the shock keeping me grounded, keeping my voice rational, calm.

"It was an arrangement."

"Are you fucking kidding me?"

"He wanted kids. That's how it started. I offered. He wanted them with you. We fell in love soon after I got pregnant with Summer, but he never stopped loving you."

"All the business trips to London, it was when you were there. He stayed with you?"

"Yes, but not all the time."

"We were at their births, for God's sake. We're their Godparents. Oh my God, Lucy, oh my fucking God."

It's the perfect deception; I would never have

suspected a thing. There were no clues. The worst thought pops into my head. “What about the girls, do they know?”

“Yes, they've always called him Pops anyway. He bought Summer and Sky a phone each, for when he was away, so the girls could speak to him. He stopped taking them when he met her.”

I pick up a mug and hurl it at the wall and watch coffee slide down the pale blue paint. I wonder who ‘her’ is. He was always helping my friend with odd jobs, at my request too. How didn't I know, how?

“Lucinda, my oldest, best friend, you pair must have had a good laugh at me, sneaking kisses behind my back.”

“It was never like that. We loved you too. That's why you couldn't find out. I loved you. Please, Rosie, I swear it was all for you.”

“How often did you sleep together?”

“Not often. More recently, not at all.”

“You need to be brave now Rosie, there's more I have to tell you.”

I slump onto the bed, staring at her face, wet with tears and broken.

“What more could there possibly be?”

“He was seeing that woman, up in Scotland; she was much younger than us. He deserved to fucking die.”

My back straightens at the sudden sharpness of her

words.

"Deserved to die? What do you mean?"

Her face changes screws up and twists. She speaks through pursed, white lips.

"That's right. He was cheating on us both, the bastard. I couldn't have that. The kids were starting to miss out on his time. He told me it was over between us, that we should stop. But I found texts on his phone from that woman, flirty texts from Isabelle."

I try to stand but drop to my knees, no strength left in my brain function or physical ability. I'm dumbfounded and words will not come out, they are tangled inside. My husband. My David. My world. So, Isabelle lied to me too, one final lie, cracked open, a gaping wound that's going to hurt and probably never heal. I run to the bathroom to spew as everything begins to spin.

Cold from the floor-tiles permeates my cheek and my speech slurs, words slide out sideways, as I try to speak. Lucinda's at my side, always at my side. Her lips move, but there's no sound. The tap dripping into the bathroom sink starts the whistling again and the church bells stop. I know it's time.

TWENTY FIVE ~ Dripping

The dripping noise is loud, suffocating, terrifying. Darkness begins. I slip into unconsciousness, uneasily, not wanting to go to the fathomless place. Nightfall comes as swiftly as an executioner's blade. It's the rhythm of water that finally allows me to see myself as a six-year-old child, my missing part, stood in rags, clutching a toy dog.

My mum is in the room, sat at the dining table under the window, with sun lighting her auburn curls gold. Her white, cotton dress is covered in tiny, yellow primroses, draping at the sides of her stocking-covered legs in pretty, pleated folds. There is a white ceramic water jug filled with peach and pink lilies on the windowsill, stripy and bold. Me and the daughter of my mum's bridge friend, Lucy, are playing with our dolls on the floor.

My mum's watching over us, over me, her eyes warning me, sipping loudly on her tea. She praises my small freckle -faced friend and I pull the head off my doll, anything to get my mum's attention.

"Why, Lucy, that's lovely. Can you make your dolly dance too?" Her voice is kind, gentle, because she is not talking to me. She flicks her eyes at me, letting me know I'm being watched.

"Rosie, go to your room now. There's a good girl." My anger is tangible, and she knows it too. She enjoys igniting my inner-turmoil and spinning me out of control, so she can cane me, six times, back of the legs, hard. Every time I have Lucy over, the groomed elegant Lucy, she treats her like a princess because her father is present in her life and is a good man. I'm sure that's it. My dad is rotten, a no good, rapist liar. That's what she likes to remind me. Although I don't know what that means, I know it's wrong, like me, wrong.

"You're just like him, ugly, inside and out." And she would pinch my inner arm or thigh, nip me where it hurt, but would never be seen.

Lucy would be with my mum. I could hear them through the floorboards. I would lie with my ear to the dusty floor, listening to their tinkling laughter and my mum's kindness. She only invited Lucy over, so she could tease me, break me, and teach me a lesson in good manners and how to be the perfect daughter. My mum was immaculately turned out. She was an elegant woman, admired, beautiful, and wrinkle free. She wore pale powder from a rose-encrusted compact that she would constantly pat across her nose and red lipstick; a wartime glamour girl, a film star. Her dresses were soft and pretty. She dressed me in old dresses that were dull from over- washing and they were void of frills or flowery patterns. They were plain, just like me.

"Plain as a peg, you are, Rosie, and not made for pretty things," she would say and laugh as she closed my bedroom door and clicked the key in the lock. I spent most of my days in that room with no toys, or books, just my imagination, thoughts, and ever-growing bitterness toward a mum that hated me with every inch of her being. She would let me out when she had people over, washed me with rags, dressed me up, and curled my wild hair into submission. She was good at playing mother and would warn me about devouring the sandwiches and cake, but she had starved me for days. I would sit and look at the food, all laid out pretty on cake stands and paper doilies. I could take one cake, one sandwich, and a small glass of lemonade. I was made to take small bites as my stomach growled with hunger. If I managed to take a few extra and stuff them in my pocket, it was fruitless because I would be searched and caned before my return to the bedroom.

"Thieving little bastard, just what I'd expect from the child of a rapist." I didn't know what a rapist was, but I suspected it was horrid.

"Don't you rush now, Rosie, ladies don't rush their food," she would say in front of her fancy friends, smiling at me the way I wish she would normally. As soon as the house was empty, she would say one word, "Room!" And there I would stay until she saw fit to feed me a morsel of blue-spotted bread or meagre scraps, just enough to keep me alive. There was never bath time, no bedtime stories, no love, nothing. I would spend time looking out of the window at the back garden. Watching the light fading at the end of the day and shade passing over the lawn, the changing light throwing lines across the floorboards. I would watch the shadows on the wall at night and hear all the sounds that other children don't notice, to me they were like music.

I learned there is no such thing as silence, owls yes, and insects, creaking pipes, distant traffic, distant music, wind, rain drumming on the window, airplanes going to faraway places, children's chiming laughter, chatting voices, shuffling, banging, and air. In the still of the summer night, even the air had its own noise, a quiet shushing sound. Those noises kept me entertained and alive. I would imagine myself in all these situations, lost in a sunny place, at a summer party, in a happy home, playing with my imaginary dog, on a plane to Peru, to live with Paddington Bear. My imagination kept me alive. I had a pet dog, a chocolate Labrador; it was really the neighbour's dog. It would bark, and bark and I would answer and answer, quietly.

I loved watching him play in the garden, free and full of bullish mischief, the neighbours named him Mowgli.

One day, Mum invited Lucy over to play and miraculously, we were allowed out into the garden. I wandered around, letting my fingers run through the grass, the flowers, all forms of buoyant garden life. I ran over to the fence to meet Mowgli in person. He came and stuck his wet nose through the chicken- wire fence, like he knew. He whimpered and whined and jumped around in circles. Lucy was moody and complained that I was ignoring her. She was shouting to my mum, who was busy in the kitchen talking on the phone. I was in Heaven, unleashed, and I contemplated escaping through the garden gate and running, just running.

We had a moss-covered water well at the bottom of the garden behind a small orchard of apple trees. I dragged her there by her arm to stop her from shouting because to lose this morsel of freedom, would have been like dying.

"Alright, Lucy, stop it! She'll make us go inside." I held her arm tightly and her face pinched together in pain. She acted like a spoiled brat, pulled her arms away and folded them across her chest.

"I don't care. I don't want to play with you anyway. You're smelly and dirty." She squinted pretty blues eyes at me and I filled with rage as she continued to shout and snigger, trying to get Mum's attention. I placed my hand across her mouth and pulled her to the wall, out of sight. I threw her to the ground. She screamed like brats do and I hit her with a small rock, on the back of the head, just once, to shut her up and stop her spoiling my day. She did too. She shut up and went limp. She looked awake and jerked a couple of times, propped against the stone wall. A trickle of blood came over her eye and down her cheek. I jumped back, so it didn't touch my white socks. Mum would scold me if I got them dirty. Lucy lay partially slumped against the wall, but was slipping down, eyes open like a doll, and then blood oozed from the corner of her mouth. I watched it for what seemed like an eternity, until it reached her chin. I was glad she was quiet but feared what my mum would do.

"Lucy, I'm sorry, get up, please." Once I knew she wasn't going to answer, I shook, and panic rose in my throat, rendering me speechless. I dragged her limp body up over the well wall and rolled her across the top, careful to stay blood-free. I struggled to move her. She was heavier than Mum's potato sack and I tripped over the very stone that killed her, hitting my head on a jagged corner. I still have the scar, the scar of a murderer, which ironically, is formed like the letter L.

I pushed her into the well and threw the stone in after. The sound of the splash when she hit the bottom was as loud as a crashing wave. The echo of it seared through my head, loud and final. I sat for a while after, listening to the drip of water. Mum was right. I was evil after all, the Devil's spawn. Mowgli howled next door as if he'd been kicked. I think he knew. He smelled death.

I ran up to the house and said to my mum, “Lucy’s ran away, Mum. She’s gone.” Mum looked horrified and put me over a kitchen chair and caned me until I couldn’t walk. It was her worst move, her biggest mistake. I watched the shadow of her arm grow on the kitchen wall; a monster, with every rise of the cane, but I deserved it. I was evil, the daughter of a rapist, ugly and unloved.

“You stupid girl, useless, useless, useless.” With every sting of the beating, she said it over and over as if getting pleasure from her demonic rhythm of torture. I was locked in my room after and lay on my side, so the blood didn’t stick to my best dress. I lay with my ear to the floor to glean what I could through the cracks in the floorboards.

I heard Lucy’s mum screaming at my mum “How could you lose her?” I heard the police asking my mum questions, for two days and two nights. I watched them search the neighbourhood, and then the garden, with torches, saw them pull Lucy from the well, covered in leeches, eyes wide open. I saw my mum handcuffed and lead into the back of a police car.

Then, I heard whistling.

The sad-sounding melody made every hair on my body stand up and I shuffled myself into a corner, under the darkest shadow, to hide. The noise came up the stairs, melancholy, eerie. A startled blackbird flew off my windowsill and the Sunday church bells chimed, way off in the distance. The steps advancing toward my room were thunderous, loud and heavy. I sat very still as I waited to meet the Devil because my mother told me that I was one of his children and he would come for me one day.

My bedroom door creaked open. My heart hammered so fast I was certain it was going to explode. A tall man stood in the doorway and I couldn't breathe. His face was hidden by the sun and his huge shadow stretched across the floor. I whispered, "The Whistler."

He came toward me, kneeled and smiled. I recoiled and winced because of the pain in my legs. He wore a police uniform. There was a look in his eyes that I later recognised to be a mixture of sadness and sympathy.

"It's OK now, little one. You're safe." He lifted me, gently, into his arms and I yelped out in pain. He carried me down the stairs with watery eyes.

"Look at her, the state of her legs, poor child," another policewoman shrieked in horror as she carefully wrapped me in a blanket. Mum tried to tell the police it was me, a six-year-old child, but they didn't believe her because of my horrific wounds, scars, and general scruffiness. She was labelled: 'child killer.' and locked away in a Scottish asylum to live out her days with the rest of the country's criminally insane. She befriended a young cleaner called Ida. She would listen to the mad woman's tales about her evil daughter, Rosie Love - me. Ida had a daughter called Isabelle, who would later confide in my husband.

The last sight I remember of my mother was in the back of a police car. I looked at her, hoping for at least a smile. I willed for her to just look at me with kindness, just once, but she turned from me, as she always had, with a stiff, disgusted defiance.

"Poor, poor girl. My God, that woman is evil," another police officer said, and I was safe. At last, I was safe. Somehow, I locked the story away, kept it so well hidden, even I couldn't find it. I'm convinced this is what happened. A long last, I have story of my own, a version of it anyway. Although, I'm never entirely sure. There are still questions. They usually come at night, after my perpetual nightly serum warms my insides, and I begin to dream.

TWENTY SIX ~ The Finale.

Carton Hayes is a forgotten building, a decaying mansion situated on a rocky outcrop in the Outer Hebrides. It's hidden away from society and in among the wildest, toughest terrain. A place impossible to escape from and now, only occupied by a few of the country's most prolific mental health cases, the last remaining nuts, not cracked by any psychiatrist. The patients that were left behind as experimental subjects with no family to interfere, the ones too far gone for anyone to care about them. Doctor *Ewan* Beckett had privately funded the project and Dr. *Lucinda* Hayden, his assistant, was only too willing to be near him at the back of beyond, where she could have his full attention and impress him with her embellished weekly reports about her pioneering ways of working with the imbeciles.

She had torturous methods of mental abuse, using a serum they used in the olden-days, containing all kinds of experimental cocktails - variations from Laudanum, Aconite (Wolfbane), Opium, Morphine, toxic Mercury and Chloral Hydrate. Some barbiturates had terrible side effects including addiction, hallucinations, and a beneficial deep sleep that enabled unorthodox methods of therapy. They employed a small number of idiot staff from a nearby village, sworn to secrecy for a handsome fee, and those staff were handed a fake nurse's uniform upon their arrival.

The gardens are overgrown, a rambling maze of uninviting gorse bushes. Coarse nettles and weeds skulk around a once magnificent iron fence, now rusting and corroded from over a century of sea air. It's a long boat trip away from civilisation and far away enough for the screams to be mistaken for wailing sirens or howling winds.

On the third floor, along a bleak corridor, in the farthest room from the doctor's offices, is the room of Rosie Love. Thirty-nine-years-old. She has been a resident for the past thirty-two years. The most fascinating case the doctors and staff have ever come across.

After murdering a child of the same age, called Lucy, at her mother's residence, a small, remote cottage, location unknown, Rosie was admitted to Carton Hayes, clutching a brown toy dog she called Mowgli. Her mother refused to have her home after the incident, saying she was cursed. She was the youngest patient to have ever been diagnosed with Delusional

Paranoid Schizophrenia. The doctors come together once a week to discuss their most revered case, a fascination for them both. So much so, they had given up their respective families to live at the crumbling mansion and study her like a new species.

"Doctor Hayden, I believe you have new information about our Rosie?" Doctor Beckett says without looking up from his notes. She pushes her glasses up her nose and nervously shuffles papers around before looking up at his bulky frame.

"Yes, the drama continues," she quickly explains.

"Do proceed, Lucinda."

"Rosie has become increasingly agitated in recent weeks, as you know. She continues to refer to her imaginary friend as Lucy or Lucinda, often blurring the lines of reality between myself and the child she murdered. She persists with the friendship, talking to her or them often. She's kept the dead child with her all these years. Each session becomes a new chapter in her fictional world. It unravels in interesting segments. It's even extended to trips away with incredible accuracy. I've never experienced anything like it. It's almost as if she's been there, which we know is impossible."

"Do you have the recordings from the last session? I'll catch up with them later."

"Yes, of course. Rosie is fusing her past and present and in such a chilling way, it's quite extraordinary."

"There's nothing ordinary about our girl. Is she still talking about the dead husband?"

"Yes, after the death of our nurse David, she has included him as a new dimension in her world. She believes that this is her life today, that she's grieving, and it's brought on a shift in her imaginary relationship with Lucy."

"How so?"

"There are signs of mistrust and there have been a number of anger eruptions against staff. She's been given PRN medicines numerous times. We've had to increase the dose. We are monitoring her behaviour closely and adjusting her nightly medications to suit."

"Make sure she's not too out of it. We still need her lucid enough to cooperate during the sessions."

"Of course." He looks directly at her and smiles, wrinkling his nose at the bridge. "And please make sure you add the transcripts to our handwritten notebook. I like to see the stories in print."

"So, tell me, when you question her about her childhood, is there any recognition?"

"No, she still refuses to talk. She will only talk about her fictional life. Before the age of seven, there is a wall of silence."

"Do you think she genuinely doesn't remember?"

"It's a classic trait. Post-traumatic stress has caused her to bury it. Most cases, especially after so many years of therapy, will release some information, enough to form a picture, sometimes only an outline. But, not our Rose. I think she'll die with her secrets."

"Did you collect the family photographs after her mother's passing at the residential home?"

"Yes, and we figured out why the two young girls in her fictional world are named Summer and Sky. Her mother owned a cottage in Wales called, '*Summer Sky*.' I didn't make the connection until I saw the photo."

"That would explain her fixation with her home being in Wales. It also confirms that her past is in that labyrinth of a head, somewhere, locked away. If only we had the key."

"Is Nurse Karen alright, after the attack? That was a nasty scar on her cheek."

"Yes, she's on the mend: however, we need to keep her as far away from Rose as possible. She's taken a real disliking to her."

"Did you hear anything back from old Nurse Jenkins? I can't believe he tried to sexually assault Rose. Because of our condemning secrecy act, we can't even prosecute the bastard, but we can move him to the male quarters. That should keep him out of trouble."

"Well, Lucy took her own revenge. That missing chunk from his arm might make him think twice before taking advantage ever again."

"We must keep a close eye on him. Tell me, does

Nurse Karen wish to remain on the wing?"

"Nurse Karen's better, but has refused to treat Rose, for the time being. It must have been terrifying. Rose was convinced that she was Nurse David's sister. I've never seen her so savage-like. She's become quite beastly."

"Hmm, OK. Will Nurse Anna see to her for a while?"

"Yes, and we've taken on Anna's son, Tom, as an orderly. He's offered to help with her treatment."

"Has he been through screening? Remember, discretion is very important."

"Of course, the usual, and he's signed the disclaimer."

"Good, good. I hear there's a new character in Rose's world?"

"Yes, she keeps mumbling about a woman called, Isabelle, insists there has been a visit, but there's no direction with that conversation yet. I don't know of an Isabelle that she's had contact with in here. It's most unusual for her to invent a person. It's usually either someone she's met or that she's heard staff talking about. This is a brand-new development. I've asked all of the staff if they have mentioned the name to her, but nobody has."

"Ah, very interesting. I do enjoy her little twists, fascinating. Do you believe that we should be doing the sessions without her straight jacket? Is she calm enough now to be in the room without wearing one?"

"I would say no, not at present. She is presenting with delusional psychosis, stronger than ever and explosive anger outbursts. It's not advisable. She seems constantly, deeply troubled, more than I've ever seen. She's also getting bad scarring on her wrists and neck where she tries to wriggle out of it."

"Okay, see that Nurse Anna treats Rose for any new, open wounds. That about sums it up. Shall we go and see our girl?"

They travel along a network of shabby, damp corridors, duck-egg-blue paint bubbling over crumbling plaster in the corners. Heavy-set nurses follow behind, one of them carrying a straitjacket. A red-light buzz as they pass through a series of heavy, bolted doors. The jangle and clank of a large bunch of keys echoes to her and she knows they're coming.

Rose is sitting in the window hollow, gripping the bars, clutching her toy dog Mowgli. She is looking out at the overgrown garden below and beyond that, the volcanic black rocks that spit white foam, and beyond them, a sea she only ever hears. Her head is shaven. Scars zigzag across her forehead and temples from old lobotomies and repeated shock therapy. There's a deep L-shaped scar above her left eye. Her eyes are haunting, dark blue, her skin moonlit-pale, almost iridescent, like she's been underground forever. Her soul is trapped inside an emaciated body. She refuses to eat most days.

Cameras at the far corners of the room focus in on her as the doctors enter. It takes three nurses to wrestle her to the ground to put on her straight jacket. The doctors shift toward the door, just in case.

"Lucy, I thought I told you we aren't friends anymore," Rose says in a childlike voice, directing her arctic gaze at Doctor Lucinda Hayden.

Rose Love's session 2,223 begins.

The End.

Carla Day resides in Wales with her son and dog Lily. She has published two novels and continues to write in multiple genres. Carla studied with The Writers Bureau and has had a short thriller published in an anthology by Burning Chair Publishers. Carla enjoys hiking, being on mountain tops and eating anything that tastes of lemon. Her boots are always muddy, she can be found on mountain tops or enjoying the sunset on the beach.

Instagram: Carladay61

Facebook: Carladay02

Twitter: Carladay02

CARLA DAY

Printed in Great Britain
by Amazon